FINA

by

John Behardien

Duncurin Publishing
Duncurin.com

Copyright © 2015

All Rights Reserved – John Behardien

No part of this book may be reproduced or transmitted in any form or by any means electronic or mechanical, including photocopying, recording, taping or by any information storage retrieval system without the written permission of the publisher.

This is a work of Fiction.
Available in Paperback and e-Book.

First Published in England MMXV

Duncurin Publishing
Monton
England

Duncurin.com

ISBN : 978-09570982-9-9

Book Design : Moosey

DEDICATION

For Rodders, Nick and all the boys: Jo, Rob and Alex. With love.

WITH THANKS

My sincere thanks to the following very talented people.

Judith and Tracey: For wonderful Proof Reading and Copy Editing. Bookhelpline.co.uk

Jamie Runyan: Another super cover design@reese-winslow.com

Cover Photo: Courtesy of Istockphoto.com 'rozbyshaka'

Other Books By John Behardien

Crack In the Code
Stars' End

The Last Great Gift

Dawn Over Vancouver
All That Time Allows (for release 2016)

Final Horizon
Final Request (for release 2016)

One Life Many Moments (for release 2016/17)

Contents

Chapter I	Lucky Escape	1
Chapter II	True Station	10
Chapter III	Cards Marked	18
Chapter IV	Afterglow	30
Chapter V	Corporate Raider	36
Chapter VI	Fates Locked as One	55
Chapter VII	Ghostly Apparition	75
Chapter VIII	Moment in Paradise	84
Chapter IX	Calypso	100
Chapter X	Deception	111
Chapter XI	Sterling Effort	120
Chapter XII	Shooter	130
Chapter XIII	One True Thing	152
Chapter XIV	Springtime In Vevey	165
Chapter XV	Dragons' Breath	183
Chapter XVI	Cloak and Dagger	202

Chapter 1

Lucky Escape

A bright winter's day had, all too suddenly, given way to a clear but chilly night over the old town of Geneva, Switzerland. Gathering darkness brought a brisk wind over Lake Leman as if it were trying to snuff out the towering water column of the Jet d'Eau. The imposing fountain had only been switched on that day, following a bout of intense frost. The roar of the water, all 500 litres per second, being pumped up to a height of 140 metres, could be heard from miles away.

The Swiss Alps, standing impassively in the background, held the promise of snow for the hordes of skiers arriving by air, car or rail. Double-decked express trains streamed off in an endless procession to convey the aficionados to the large ski resorts of Wengen, Zermatt, and Verbier. Intense arc lights of the piste bashers, could be seen from a great distance, going about their lonely work throughout the night, repairing and renovating hundreds of ski runs.

The young couple had just left their favourite restaurant 'Le Petit Cochon' on the north shore of Lake Geneva. Despite the cold night, the pair lingered on the poorly lit pavement. The woman draped her arms around her companion pulling him down. The extra weight caused him to wobble uncertainly. Her short shift dress rode up just a little as he hugged round her waist. Playfully, she flexed her left knee behind her as she used more of her weight to pull him towards her to kiss him. His efforts at staying upright meant that he didn't see the tall figure, dressed in black, appear behind them until it was too late.

The stranger moved quietly but remained hidden in the shadows until he was ready to act. It was not until he was in the glare of the headlights of a large, black Mercedes that the young man sensed danger. Suspecting the car was about to mount the pavement, he dropped his girlfriend defensively. Her spiky heels skidded precariously over the moist pavement and she struggled to get her balance after losing the support of his neck. Her shock, as she faced the twin tasks of reacting to being let go in this way and being flooded in the harsh light from the car's full beam, was denoted by a gasp from her lush red lips, together with a hastily masked expletive.

The Mercedes stopped just in front of them, its bonnet dipping as the brakes struggled against the weight of the car. The front doors opened and two darkly clothed men rushed directly towards them. Both figures sported black balaclavas and approached with an air of menace. Only then did the lovers understand the danger they were in. The young man instinctively turned away from the approaching men, reaching for his girlfriend's hand as he did so. However, the unseen man now appeared behind them as they sought escape, effectively blocking their route.

"In the car. Now!" he instructed, his face being disguised by a pair of black Bollé ski goggles. "I ain't askin' agin."

One of the men opened the rear door and the young couple were manhandled with sufficient force to prevent either protest or delay. Two men took the front seats and the third joined the terrified pair. For the moment, the waving of a large, weighty pistol in their direction unequivocally precluded the need for speech.

A few moments later the young male tried to speak as the girl sobbed uncontrollably.

"What do you want with us?" he exclaimed into the confines of the car, just before the man in the front passenger seat turned round and covered their heads, in turn, with black cotton bags. He used enough force to effectively silence any protest, apart from the howling that continued to wail from her lips.

As the vehicle sped away, heading north, the young male regained enough composure to pose a string of questions. "What do you want?" "Why us?" We are not important people; we are 'nobodies' on a night out. Just a boy and girl having a night out…," were met with stony silence, the only sound being the smoothly pulsating engine as it sped through the cold night.

From the deep shadows of a side street, a tall, slim young woman appeared. She pulled the belt of her black coat a little more tightly against the cold, her discomfort made worse by her long wait. She clicked a discreet microphone attached to her lapel and said, "Horizon control, they are on their way, activate phase two." Message delivered, she quickly walked along the slippery pavement running alongside the lake, in order to find her parked car.

Some time later the black Mercedes approached a deserted warehouse on an industrial complex due north of the city. A fourth man also wearing black clothing and a balaclava awaited them. Having a quick cigarette, he was galvanised into action as soon as he heard the engine. He rushed to open a large door and the car sped in, its front end dipping once again with the precipitous nature of the halt. Gazing around conspiratorially to make sure they had not been followed, he then closed the door behind them. The abductees were dragged from the black saloon, the girl's weeping rising to a crescendo with her rough handling. They were sat unceremoniously on to two large metal chairs and handcuffed to the frames. Hoods were removed and finally, they could see their captors standing before them. All wore balaclavas apart from one, to whom the others seemed to defer, who retained his ski goggles.

The young man tried to speak again, addressing himself to the man in the goggles. "What do you want with us? We're an ordinary couple."

"Na, don't fink so, sonny. We rekkon yew two are gud for a million any day ov the week, and I fink, for us at least, it's payday! That is, if your folks cough the cash, wivout delay, or weel just 'ave ta drop you boaf, quite litrally ov course, in Lake Geniva." He laughed, taking delight in his own words. "Bit ov water, covers a load a sins, that's wot I alwiz saiz." He laughed again.

Having continued to wail for some time, the young woman suddenly had an absolute gem of an idea. She'd always been able to think quickly in a tight spot and mercifully this attribute had not deserted her. Within seconds of her mind processing the idea, she stopped sobbing, realising that an opportunity for escape had opened up.

Her voice appeared a little shrill at first while she desperately fought to calm it. "Look, my parents are penniless, so it's no use keeping me."

"But Annabelle, you told me that your Dad is Lord Calvington."

She ignored her partner at that juncture: for her plan involved only saving herself.

"Look," she began again, her tawny eyes like beads staring at the leader of the men, doing her best to stare earnestly at him. He remained impassive behind the smooth-black finish of the goggles. "His Dad's loaded. He's the one you want."

"Annabelle!"

Continuing to ignore him, she went on, "A million is chickenfeed to his Dad. He's well minted, owns his own software company and loads of other things. I'd ask for more, if I were you. I'm only with him 'cause he's filthy rich, but he's lousy in bed and he snores like a bear with flu." She offered this as further validation, now nodding to her captor as if expecting him to have knowledge of this.

"Annabelle!"

"Just let me go." Her voice was even more entreating, as she pushed her bargain for all she was worth. "Keep him, it'll be easier for you, and you'll get as much as you want from his old fella." Her accent steadily slipping from its previous more clipped tones.

"But Annabelle, all those things you told me."

"It's like this, Darion, there's no point in both of us getting hurt, now is there? Sorry, 'n all that," her enunciation continued to change, "but my Dad's an out of work refuse collector in Sheffield."

"So, you didn't go to Roedean? And you haven't just come from finishing school in Villars?"

Her expression conveyed far more than mere words ever could.

His mouth opened as a fish's struggling out of water, but in any event, only disappointment and betrayal could have ever found a voice there.

She continued to work the silence. "So, how about it? Let me go, and I won't say a word. Blindfold me and perhaps drop me *off* somewhere on the north shore of the lake, and you'll have my silence. His Dad's always bailing him out; in fact, ask for a million *pounds*, not *euros*. Bernard Pollofino, that's him, just Google him, like I did."

She prattled on for a little while longer, but eventually her words had finished, and simply the confident, beseeching look lingered – a look that only one who believed she'd presented a compelling case for release could generate.

The men glanced at each other and the three especially towards their leader. Darion was completely silent now having been subsumed totally by the misery etched indelibly to his face. Unable to contemplate the thought that the men would kill him, he knew, too, that his Dad would almost certainly bail him out – again. There'd be the usual lecture, of course; the initial rage would be followed soon after, by that inevitable disappointment in his eyes.

Darion's long fingers fumbled with the hinged case in his pocket containing the square-cut, brilliant-white diamond engagement ring that he'd been planning to present that night. How lucky he'd been, for his consort was evidently not the person he thought. Reflecting on this, he considered that it was a solitary bright spot on an otherwise bleak vista, which contained many more unhappy ones. Invariably, everything he touched fell apart in his hands. No doubt there would be other rich pickings for her: there was an abundance of rich men, or the children of such men, frequenting the clubs, bars and casinos of Geneva.

The lead kidnapper, who snapped his fingers and pointed to the girl, interrupted his bleak mood. His accomplices understood immediately and readied the bag to slip over her head. She would not gaze at her ex-lover again. However, she did glance at the leader of the gang who used his index finger to draw across his own throat as one would a sharp knife, before using the same finger to point to the young man. Darion pulled himself up to his full height, straightening his spine as he did so. Whatever now awaited him, he knew that he wasn't going to moan and he wasn't going to beg. Perhaps, on the simplest level, he realised, in those final few minutes that he deserved this fate. People had told him so many times that he was wasting his life and that he could be more productive. His failure to heed such advice was surely what was being visited on him now.

Annabelle sighed with relief at the thought of the kidnapper accepting her perfectly valid argument. Knowing that freedom would be only moments away, she quietly congratulated herself just as the bag was used to cover her head. Given that she was on her way back to the city, she'd ask to be dropped off where she'd been taken because the nightclubs were still in full swing and there were many more people to meet. She was guided into the back of the car; she heard the warehouse door being opened carefully for the car to drive through. Within seconds the Mercedes departed again into the cold but still night. Only a slight burbling noise came from the exhaust, before the engine took up its weight, and it accelerated away.

The black saloon was soon swallowed by the darkness, setting a course bound for the north shore of the lake, and her freedom. As the car made more progress she was already busily planning her next rich, but foolish conquest. It was always said that a fool and his money were soon parted and she understood this maxim, for it ran through every vein in her body.

One of the remaining kidnappers closed the motorised door to the industrial unit, which looked so much larger and desolate, given the space being vacated by the car. The solitary, but valuable, hostage sat there, crestfallen, as he agonised over what would be the next disaster to overtake him.

Moments later, four large black vans crept carefully on the Tarmacadam outside the warehouses. Using the lowest engine power, just enough to propel them forwards, whilst keeping sound levels to a minimum, they halted a few metres away. Each van was filled to capacity with men dressed totally in black. No lights were visible, but some of the men had night-vision equipment, activated just before the leading van stopped. Making their exit quietly and stealthily, they addressed themselves to the warehouse door, two to each side, carefully placing plastic charges at key points around the entrance.

Having done this, the four men retreated to a safe position either side of the frame, which was now rigged to explode. Thirty more men exited quickly and quietly from the other vans. All were dressed in similar black combat gear. The second, larger group took up strategic positions without delay but at a safe distance from the primed explosives. Rifles were presented and stun grenades were made ready.

The charges blew, making surprisingly little noise, but the door, being fatally compromised, fell away, having been knocked out of its retaining frame with a sharp shriek of metal on metal. This was the only signal needed for the men to surge forward. Rushing into the warehouse, they found three startled kidnappers and an even more surprised hostage. No fewer than thirty assault rifles were now pointed at the four men. The three kidnappers raised their arms above their heads before plastic ties restrained them. One man, slightly shorter, but more thickset than the others, stepped forward confidently. Wearing body armour, he carried no weapon and no helmet, sporting instead a black beret with a chequered black and white band around its rim. Before he spoke, two other men advanced; quickly but thoroughly, patting down the hostage for weapons or any explosive charges.

"Darion Pollofino?" asked the man in the beret.

Darion awoke from his shock in time to answer, "Yes, that's me." The misery on his face had paradoxically been made worse by his rescue. This was one more thing he'd neither asked for, nor was deserving of.

"You are safe now, Mr Pollofino. We'll have you out of here, and on your way home, in a few minutes. Our private security force has been retained by Interpol, and we've been tracking this gang for months. As soon as the car arrives, we will take you to a destination of your choice."

Although this was the third shock that the twenty-six-year-old had faced that day, the latter paled in comparison with being abducted and even more so beside the abandonment and betrayal by the woman he regarded as a steady girlfriend. One who'd promptly ditched him, in order to save her own hide, with next to no hesitation whatsoever. Notwithstanding this, relief broke out on his face, although briefly, as he contemplated the more pressing thoughts that he would have to address in the days ahead.

Chapter II

True Station in Life

Some days later, the slim, svelte and toned woman was eventually shown into the businessman's office, having been waiting for him for at least thirty minutes. She knew that rich, powerful men, in particular, had their foibles, their need to remind lesser people of their true station in life. Her acceptance of such matters was not only borne out of years of experience in dealing with such people, but also the overarching knowledge, to which all else paled, was that he owed them, in every sense of the word. A somewhat subservient and cowed secretary opened the double doors in dark, polished oak. The imposing room was lined with bookcases, and in turn her eyes were drawn forward to a matching impactful twin-pedestal desk. This appeared to have been raised even higher from the floor and the man she'd come to meet sat there, silhouetted against the available light.

The dark-grey pencil skirt she wore looked demure but attractive. A shiny belt demarcated it from the black and white animal print shirt. The whole ensemble was completed by spiky, black patent shoes, which clipped satisfyingly on the oak flooring. As was her style, she made her way through the long office with easy confidence.

He studied the young woman intently and appeared more than a little disappointed that there was neither cleavage nor much of her legs on show. Sensing the direction of his thoughts, she coughed to focus his mind on the reason for her visit. She sat on the chair that he'd pointed towards and, despite the tight skirt, somehow managed to cross her legs, each silky limb swishing gently against each other. Although her shaped blouse was buttoned almost to the top, it seemed that her chest, for now, drew the focus of his vision. As she spoke clearly and concisely, his gaze was only distracted momentarily to her eyes. Taking advantage of this temporary shift in his attention, she took the opportunity to smile at him.

"Thank you for seeing me, Mr Pollofino."

"May I congratulate you and your team on a wonderful job, Miss Clancy," he began.

"Thank you, Mr Pollofino, we aim to please."

Using a slight pause, whilst he surveyed her again, she retrieved her slim case from the floor and placed it on her lap. He couldn't help but stare as he noticed the amazing object. It was machined from two identical slabs of pure aluminium. Concealed pivots had been crafted in each base so that the two halves hinged perfectly, but invisibly, together. The whole thing was light, slim but immensely strong. His eyes continued with their fascination for the attaché. Long index fingers were deployed as she lightly touched the two dark panels on either side of the top of the case. After scanning her fingerprints, the mechanism that unlocked it stirred into life with a quiet but noticeable whirring noise. Somehow a gap formed between the flawless halves as it opened, revealing a single piece of paper. His line of vision and his interest had been captured totally by the beautiful valise.

Smiling gently in his direction, she knew that he was not looking at her. 'They always go for the case,' she thought. 'I wondered if that might distract him a bit. Men always go for the case. What is it about the case?'

She retrieved a single sided sheet of A4 paper, the invoice she was there to have settled, and gave it to him. Only a momentary flicker from one eyebrow betrayed any emotion on his otherwise impassive features as he tried to hide his mounting fascination with his visitor. Rich people never revealed the slightest interest in ordinary folk. There was an unwritten, but universal rule that applied to all such people; he tried to rein in his curiosity and the queries that bubbled restlessly within.

Suddenly, without warning his emotions overpowered him and the questions began.
"How did you know she would rat on him in that way? Was it simply luck?"

Her features sharpened a little, although she made an effort to remove the frustration in her reply. "Mr Pollofino, we promised you a result. If I may remind you, we like to feel that we are experts in the service we offer clients. We strive to be very good at what we do, with meticulous research and planning as well as rehearsals for each stage of our operations. We try not to resort to 'luck'. We knew, for instance, that the woman was not who she made herself out to be, and has an extensive history of, shall we say, entrapping rich young men, like your son, for material gain. Having gleaned this information, all we then needed to do, in this fairly simple operation, was to give her the opportunity to reveal her true colours."

"Well, it worked beyond my wildest dreams. Darion has returned to the UK and wants to start *work*," he offered with a delighted emphasis, "in one of our family businesses. He says his wild days are over and it's time to 'man up' about life."

"As I said before, Mr Pollofino, we aim to please."

She just knew there'd be something else; with rich people, there was always something.

He continued, "Tell me though," tapping the invoice a little irritatedly, "did you really need no fewer than forty SWAT members in your 'rescue' team?"

"We use whatever resources we feel we need in order to, where possible, guarantee a favourable outcome, and also to ensure authenticity at all times. If you'd have wanted a cut-price service, then, perhaps, there are others you could have retained?"

She smiled and, without doubt, there were so many things that could be said under cover of a dazzling smile, just like the one he had just witnessed. One that was also useful for hiding deeper thoughts, as she mused, privately, 'This is the thing about rich people, always wanting the outcome, but can't help but wonder if it could've been delivered at a cheaper price.'

He stirred from his lifelong, habitual, mean instincts, and now offered a conciliatory grin of his own.

"Forgive me, I assured you, when I engaged your team, that cost was not an issue. I just wanted my son back, and this is what you've given me. I cannot thank you, or your team nearly enough. And as regards your other comment, I'm not aware of anyone else who could have provided anything close to the service that you have. Tell me, have you a large squad?" Having repressed such emotions for so long, his curiosity was now overflowing.

"I'm not at liberty to discuss this with you, but I can say that we recruit, retain and sometimes also engage those with the specialist and discerning skills required to bring about a specific, successful outcome."

"But you never advertise?" he asked, incredulously.

"We have no need to advertise," she assured him, now with an enigmatic but indulgent twinkle crossing her face. "Sadly, there are many wealthy businessmen, like you, whose children have, shall we say, made unfortunate choices. We aim, as you are aware, where possible, to correct these problems."

"But, how do people get to learn about you, if you don't advertise?"

"We need to remain discrete. If we reveal the nature and the depth of services we are able to provide, then, we may jeopardise a mission and risk alienating or endangering those we try to save. This is why we insist on confidentiality, absolute secrecy and why, of course, your son must never know that he was at no point in danger and wasn't really rescued in the nick of time by a SWAT team."

"Quite so!" He laughed, as he finally warmed to his young visitor. "Forgive my curiosity, I know when we first met, you said that you could offer me solutions, not necessarily answers."

"Yes, indeed," she confirmed.

"I'm just surprised that a shadowy organisation like yours, can attract enough fee-paying clients. I suppose it's the businessman in me, always calculating the margin."

Once again, a dazzling, rather than indulgent smile served as more than sufficient a reply.

Sensing that their meeting was drawing to a close, he pulled on a shallow but wide desk drawer, and retrieved an impactful chequebook, which he opened towards her, as one might a sketchpad.

He spoke as he wrote. The thick gauge paper, embossed with his company's logo, was a little unruly, so a thick wrist and broad hand were used to subdue it while he made it out. She saw the large flourishing movements from his fingers as the Starwalker fountain-ink pen was dragged over the watermarked, high security paper.

'Another hallmark of the rich,' she thought, 'flowing calligraphy making up their signature.'

"This is from my personal account and I have included a significant bonus, in recognition of a successful and pleasing outcome."

Receiving the cheque, her pink lips sparkled, the smile still dancing with delight on her clear features, as she looked at him.

Holding open the aluminium case, she was about to drop the cheque inside. Just before she did so, however, she noted his persistent fascination for the sleek slabs of pure elemental metal. She swore that he licked his lips as he looked upon it.

"That's so kind of you, Mr Pollofino." He was rewarded, once again, with the effulgent smile and sparkle from her deep brown eyes, which resembled discs of polished Cuban Mahogany, while they surveyed him steadily. Rather than allow the cheque to fall within the confines of the attaché, she clasped her long fingers carefully around the paper, in order to fold it precisely in half. Simultaneously, with her other hand, she inserted a finger between the halves of the case so as to prevent it closing. A further swish of smooth flesh on flesh occurred, as she uncrossed her legs, and stood. Continuing to hold the cheque, she leant forwards to offer him the object of his absolute enthralment. Smiling again, she thought, 'They always want the case!'

"Please don't allow it to close, until you have reset the fingerprint decoder; there are instructions inside," she advised.

He gratefully, but carefully received it as one might a delicate, priceless piece of earthenware. The look on his face, however, was more that of a small boy who'd just been told it was okay to stroke the puppy.

She formed a handshake with her free hand. Setting down his new possession, he grasped her fingers eagerly but gently, now a very different person from the one she'd encountered at the outset. Providing a little nod and a smile, she turned. The visitor held her head erect and her spine straight while she walked confidently the way she'd come, without looking back. He stood, also, as she did, albeit still staring at the case. He deliberately delayed further examination of it, for he realised that he had one task that was even more pressing. Waiting until he heard his secretary showing her out of his offices, he then directed his attention elsewhere.

Picking up the telephone handset on his desk, he dabbed at the numbers with urgency.
"Michael, it's Bernard, here. She's just gone. They've delivered! What a brilliant result, beyond my wildest dreams. Not cheap, of course, but then again… Here is the number. You can ring at any time. When you phone, you will hear only a short tone. At that point, please say nothing other than 'new

horizon' and then just put the phone down. They will subsequently make contact with you within 24 hours. Good luck, and I hope they can do for you what they've done for me and for Darion. Goodbye."

It was only as he went to bed that night that he realised with a laugh, exactly why they had no need to advertise. Had Miss Clancy been there, she might have thought that even the most business-savvy brains were not necessarily the sharpest. In any event, the maxim that 'one positive comment was worth a thousand adverts', was very much in force.

Chapter III

Cards Marked

The tall, elegant woman walked into the casino. Heads turned in her direction as she did so. Looking straight ahead, it appeared that she refused eye contact with everyone she passed. An observant person, however, would have noticed the croupier at the roulette table, nearest the path of her travel, nod almost imperceptibly as she went by. Very astute observers may have noticed six other men and women, who were dotted around the room, do exactly the same. Continuing to smile outwardly to all who looked upon her, she confidently made her way to the rear of the room. She barely paused at what appeared to be a blank wall. Hearing an expected slight click, her hand came forward to push against the door-sized panel, which was hidden, between the raised features of the wall's decorative moulding. The croupier, who'd activated the switch, glanced back only for a moment to make sure that she'd gained access. Her slim frame slipped unobtrusively through the concealed doorway as she passed directly into the corridor beyond. Even a close and interested onlooker could have blinked and missed completely her transit through the hidden portal.

Venturing forth, she came to a smoky but brightly lit room. She looked up at the unusual lights mounted in an array on the ceiling. For the moment, she ignored three of the men seated at the card table. The stranger looked directly at the large man with the glasses, furthest away, but directly facing her. He was a bloated, bulky man with a shiny pink complexion and an even pinker and shinier nose. Smoking profusely, he was partially obscured by the fog given off by his rancid cigarette. He sported a dark blazer and an open-necked shirt, which would never have fastened across his thick neck, one that was so short as to be almost absent. The smoker looked up casually, almost unconcernedly, as he blew smoke in the direction of his young opponent who was sitting diagonally opposite him.

The young player in the designer, long-sleeved shirt looked sweaty and nervous, feverishly clutching cards that, he somehow knew, signified certain ruin. Moreover, he continued to slip one over the other as he stared, desperately hoping that by doing so, he would magically change their denomination. Despite his surprise at the entry of the strikingly attractive woman, disbelief remained the dominant emotion on his face as he wondered just how things could have gone so badly wrong. Further contemplation of a losing streak that had left him in debt to the large man in the blazer to the tune of over half a million, sterling.

The large man spoke, but was either unable or unwilling to exclude condescension or ridicule that modulated his gravelly voice, suggesting that this was the way he spoke to most people – and women in particular.

"Are you in the wrong place, my dear? The ladies' is to the right of the bar. I'm not sure someone of your delicate constitution should be in here." He looked at the long, toned arms, the fitted, beautifully cut shift dress while he considered the lithe form within.

Her spiky heels had brought her height to within a couple of inches of the six-foot she would have needed to be able to engage him eye-to-eye. The younger card player offered further, more friendly advice.

"I wouldn't stay in here. It's not a nice place for a girl like you." He pointed to the security men who, though wearing suits, couldn't have hinted more firmly that their sartorial choice was completely at variance with their real role. She smiled briefly but didn't look at the young man. Only after a palpable delay did she speak, addressing herself to him but still without looking in his direction.

"You might wish to remain quiet until the grown-ups have finished their business."

The big man stood up. Unabridged irritation now replaced the casual indifference he showed moments before.

"About time you stood for a lady," she fired in his direction.

"You impudent whore," he returned. How she hated that word. He reached for his belt as if he were about to remove it, but merely adjusted it over his ample girth. Sadly for him, in adjusting the belt, the large metal buckle dipped below his paunch rather than being hoisted upwards. The remaining two card players stayed seated as if their presence there was merely window-dressing to the main event. The tension in the room became more charged; the security guards stiffened, now coming forwards to stand a little way behind their boss. One unbuttoned his jacket, the bulge from his revolver on his left side suddenly less visible. The nervous young player stood up, having become fearful as to her safety and what would befall this slim, pretty woman in that dreadful room.

Only then did she address him by name. "Tim, please stay there; in a minute I am going to ask you to leave the room, which you are to do without looking back and without making any attempt to return. Someone will be waiting for you in the main casino, as soon as you leave here. They can be trusted."

"No, he won't be doing that," came from the gravelly voice. "He owes me another one hundred thousand as of tonight's turn of the cards."

He then threw in his two pairs on to the smooth green baize of the table.

"Yes, and you knew this because you have marked all the cards in the whole deck. The smoke that you blow in quantity in his direction acts as a catalyst for the dye that has been applied to them and is then shown up by the ultraviolet emitters you have installed in the ceiling. Those glasses allow you, and you alone, to view the marks."

He laughed, but there was nothing pleasant, either in his voice, or his demeanour. "You insult me. You dare to call me a cheat in my own casino! You snivelling bitch!"

How she hated that word, too.

"Pass me the glasses, then and 'hey presto!' I will tell you what cards you have."

Deciding to say no more, he removed the spectacles and blazer. He stretched his enormous shoulders as if making ready for a wrestling match.

The woman remained icily cool, her voice dropping a register, but it did not falter. "Here's what's going to happen. He leaves, I stay." She then produced a beautiful slim aluminium case and flicked her thumbs over the two dark panels. It opened immediately, after giving off a slight whirring noise. The two guards stiffened in readiness as they wondered what she was about to remove from the gorgeous case. The one who'd unbuttoned his jacket felt his left side for reassurance that his weapon was still there. Without looking into the case and looking all the while at the bulky man, she withdrew sealed bundles of notes, which she placed on the table.

"One hundred thousand, cash, for you now, and all his debts are cancelled. You won't hear from him, or me again. You won't be harmed. But, if I do hear of you pulling a stunt like this in the future," once again, she looked at the funny lights on the ceiling, "then, I will return, and I'll be looking for you. And next time I need to visit you, I won't be in nearly as good a mood as I am tonight."

He laughed, but somehow he knew that there was nothing to laugh about and, in point of fact, his whole bodily stance was that of someone who was far from amused. Before he could speak, she then retrieved two packs of sealed and ciphered cards from inside the case. "Or, we play seven-card stud, you and me. Winner takes all. You lose, and all his debts are cancelled."

He laughed again, but his dismissal of the young woman had turned into something much more venal as he directed his eyes to attempt to pierce the fabric of her dress, endeavouring to undress her with his eyes alone.

She smiled, briefly, as if she'd been expecting this outcome all along; a repugnant, but by no means intimidated, look appeared on her face. Coming then to her final offer, the point at which they would settle their differences, having known this even before she'd walked in.
"My third and last offer is you and I, one to one. The person who can still walk out of here takes it all." Looking at the young man she suggested, "Time for you to leave, I believe, Tim." She nodded and smiled pleasantly in his direction.

Once again, the gravelly voice responded, "You'll be very lucky to be still able to walk by the time I've finished with you and I'll take the one hundred thousand *and* what he owes me, over the remains of that pretty body; only it won't be very pretty when I'm done with it."

She grinned unconcernedly. This was the quickest and easiest option for her. But at least she'd given him the other proposals that she'd been instructed to make. She offered up a flat palm in order to stall events for a moment or two. Looking down at the spiky shoes, she delicately slipped them from her feet, the hem of her dress rising tantalisingly up glossy, firm thighs as she did so. "Don't harm the Laboutins," she clarified.

Barely waiting for her to make ready, he lunged forward. Few people would have failed to be terrified by the sight of this massive, and, by now, very angry man who surged headlong like a rhinoceros making a charge. She allowed him to approach for a second or two, but his haste and overconfidence had already defeated him. Looking almost distractedly behind her as if she had all the time in the world, she made sure that she had enough room. She turned back to face him; he was almost upon her. In an instant, she rocked back on her left hip as her right leg came up. Her upper body tilted back allowing her leg to rise to the height she needed. Her arms delicately and effortlessly counterbalanced her shifting weight. The flat sole of her right foot was aimed, precisely, but devastatingly, at his solar plexus. Although he'd adjusted the overstretched belt, it still sat too low on his pendulous abdomen for the metal buckle to provide any protection. The crucial conjunction of arteries and nerves that were grouped at this spot were barely protected by the rolls of soft fat as her foot gave up its momentum with unstoppable consequences.

Pain erupted like an explosion deep at his core. His eyes bulged at the violence that was coursing through his body; his pink complexion became much redder in hue. For the moment, however, he didn't go down. Her foot was firmly planted once again and the left leg still powered her forwards. Bringing her right arm up, her elbow bent at a right angle. The intruder was ready to parry any possible incoming blow. The pain that wracked him had long since precluded any specific response. In truth he was already defeated. He tottered for a moment causing her to wonder if he'd be able to mount a last-minute lunge upon her, recognising that his bulk could still provide him with momentary, but possible, bout-winning capability. She decided to settle it beyond doubt and prepared to administer her final blow.

Her right arm remained high. Once again she rocked back using the left leg to steady herself, although now the right leg planted firmly on the floor. Transferring her weight to her forward facing foot, truncheon like, she used the edge of her entire right forearm. The sweeping blow was brought about by a brisk but powerful extension from her elbow like a literal coup de grâce as she somehow found his larynx in the very short neck. At this point, he did fall, in one leaden, spluttering sweating lump, hitting the floor as intense pain and breathlessness vied equally upon him.

Finally, the stranger turned away from him, this time to recover her expensive shoes.

Looking up, she asked the young card player, "Are you still here?"

"I thought you might need some support," he offered, laughing at the redundancy of his words. "But, perhaps, I could at least offer you some help, with the shoes!"

He provided a supporting arm while she delicately stepped back into them, the graceful movement at complete variance with that shown seconds before. The trademark red soles glinted temporarily against the polished floor as she regained her balance.

"Look!" he shouted.

One of the security guards had stepped forwards to help his felled boss who continued to cough and splutter violently, clutching his throat, while he struggled for breath. The other guard, however, had reached inside his jacket to retrieve his revolver, which he now unlocked and pointed at the woman.

She reached up almost as if she were stretching lazily. However, her movements were deceptively quick and she acted without hesitation as if she'd anticipated his intervention. Her long hair had been tied up using two slim blades, like trochars, but even sharper. She grasped first one of these with her left hand and, as her arm came down, her flexed wrist snapped with violent hyperextension launching the slim, sharp, but deadly projectile forwards, like an arrow.

It caught him full on the wrist; his dominant hand lacerated, causing the gun to fall harmlessly to the floor. As her right arm came up to retrieve the other blade, she presented her left palm, "One remaining, gentlemen, but do anything rash, and it will be in the middle of someone's forehead in a second or two." She smiled again and then offered, "Please don't make me angry, now that we've had such a nice evening. Our business, I believe, has been concluded."

She placed the cards and the money back inside the case, which immediately closed with a slight whir and a click. The black sensors blinked momentarily with the graphic of a tiny padlock, as the two immaculate halves were brought together.

The two other card players stayed seated throughout the whole exchange, now looking at each other with a mixture of fear and incredulity. She motioned for the young player to leave ahead of her and they departed. Just before doing so, she turned before entering the corridor, flicking her blade at the array of UV lights in the ceiling, which promptly fizzed, spat and shorted out. The two returned to the main room after pushing back on the concealed doorway. Only the woman's unravelled long hair, now flowing gloriously in her wake, bore testament to her recent exertions.

He scurried by her side. "Wow! Who are you?"

"Who I am, is not important."

Now leaving, she made the briefest of eye contact with several people round the room, who, upon her signal, also made preparations to go. Continuing to walk with the bedazzled card player, and upon exiting the building, she clicked a key fob, thereby illuminating a beautiful white sports car.

"Please get in," the svelte woman said.

The 5-litre petrol engine fired moments later, four exhaust pipes venting the magnificent V8 of the 'F-Type' Jaguar. She re-joined their conversation as soon as they were underway.
"Who I am isn't important. This is about who you are. It seems that you've mixed with some nasty types, who are by no means your friends."

Suddenly, he gave a little laugh and leant back in his seat as his head went back, "Oh, I see now, my father sent you!"

Once again her voice dipped by a semitone, as she struggled to make her point. "As I said, this isn't about anyone else but you."

The white car left Cannes by the coast road but then switched north. While she drove, he stared at the long legs and attractive figure of this gorgeous woman.

Sensing the direction of his gaze, she suggested, "Eyes on the road. Good job you are not driving or we'd be into the next tree," as she flicked the paddle-shifters to manually change gear.

"It's about how you are going to spend the rest of your life."

"Oh, oh, its sounds as if I'm going to get *the lecture*."

She smiled briefly but her voice had much more of an urgent tone, struggling to master her irritation, as she continued. "You can either spend it with twisting bastards, like him," she pointed over her shoulder back the way they'd come, "playing crooked card games in smoky rooms, or you can put in place one or two improvements."

"Here it is. I just knew it, *the* lecture. My Dad has given me this talking-to a few times now. He engaged you, didn't he? Story of my life, pretty girl enters the room, and my Dad has sent her! To deliver his sermon!"

He caught the flicker of her smile in the illumination from the car instruments.

"I doubt I'll be there to save you next time."

"That's a shame, I thought we could get a drink."

"Look, Tim, you can keep coming out with these cheap lines, but trust me, even you will get bored with them eventually."

The car continued north. The intense headlights illuminated the sweeping French roads. The still night air of the south had created a balmy evening, despite the time of year, and was swept in hungrily through the engine intakes.

"Eventually, you'll look back and find that your life contains absolutely nothing and probably no-one. Especially with these smarmy lines you keep trotting out."

"And yours does?" he asked with a little giggle, fed by the alcohol he'd drunk.

She smiled, flicking the paddle-shift down a gear on the 8-speed gearbox as she blipped the accelerator to raise the revs to match the lower gear. The car surged smoothly and effortlessly as it took up a higher level of speed.

"You'll be able to answer that question before you go to bed tonight."

"Will you be coming too?"

"Something tells me that you are not a very quick learner, eh, Tim? Perhaps these little quips are the only way you can break up the boredom," she said, as if she, too, had learned one more thing that night.

It was just after 1am when the open-top Jaguar came to a stop. The exhaust note changed to a satisfying burble as she stopped the car outside a luxury block of apartments in Mougins, to the north of Cannes.

"Tim, here is my company card, and if you do wish to know more, then all you have to do is to phone that number. If not, then, have a nice life, as they say, won't you? Please think about what I've said. You can live your life or you can spend it watching it go down the toilet. It's your choice. Just don't say we didn't give you a chance."

In the time taken for the drive, something of her words and her attitude was now stirring within. He seemed more reflective and, most vitally, a lot less flippant as he asked, "Excuse me, may I know your name?"

She laughed, "Yes, of course, it's not all cloak and dagger stuff, you know."

He waited for an age. "Well?"
"You'll get to know my name, if and when you phone that number," she smiled. "Goodnight, Tim." She looked away from him.

He left the car as he realised she would say nothing more. Miss Clancy pressed the accelerator and the 'F-Type' squealed a little as the electronic differentials came into force and the car shot away, before being enveloped by the still night.

It was the stunning smile, more so than her calm relaxed manner, or anything of her words, that ultimately made most impact on him. What was worse, much worse, was that she was about to leave his life, complete with those beautiful looks. He knew that the only way he would ever see her again, let alone that engaging smile, was in his hands as he studied the card she'd given him.

Chapter IV

Afterglow

The young woman returned from the window, needing to get to her feet, to walk just a little, as they went over the same ground. She looked through the large tinted windows and over the cold, uninviting waters of the Manchester Ship Canal. Her four colleagues had remained seated round the table. One of the large screens on the wall illuminated a fifth, who was communicating via videoconferencing. Going through things once again, she realised that nothing had changed, but she felt a pressing need to summarise things as being the only way to keep her sanity.

"Look, I've met with Lord Bollington. He definitely wants us to take the case," came from her male colleague on the thin but large screen.

"That's all very well," she offered, "but it's an unusual undertaking for us. What have you said to him?"

She pursed her lips together, sensing his thoughts.

He continued mocking her slightly, "Ooh, I said that we'd look at it, but couldn't promise that we'd take it on."

"It looks like a tricky one, not our usual sort of project," she agreed, and then added, "These are complex affairs. Do you remember when we started all those years ago? We promised that, unless we could be as near one hundred per cent certain we could bring about a clearly beneficial outcome for the client and the subject, we would not interfere. You realise, we have so much work on at the moment, surely we don't want to bite off more than we can chew?"

She felt compelled to pace up and down again. He found himself craning his neck round as she moved around the room even though he was looking at her via the video-link.

"Yes, I have to say I agree with you totally. Perhaps I should tell Lord 'B' that we are fully engaged at present. He won't be happy. He's not a man who likes to hear anything but 'how soon do you want it', but there we are. Go on then, put some photos up, let's see what we're about to turn down," he suggested.

She clicked a button on her handheld control, and photos cycled through one by one on another screen, visible to all.

"Well, I suppose we might as well."

"Pardon?"

"I said, 'we might as well'."

"What! Did I miss something, here? I thought I'd just heard you say something completely different. And why, might I ask, when I thought we'd all decided we could do without the headache of this type of assignment?"
Rising panic made her continue, before allowing him to speak. "Just what are we hoping to achieve here?" she asked with prescience. "I just have a bad feeling about it all."

"We might as well take it on. You know how I don't like to let clients down. No, I think we'll do it."

"Pardon me, is there someone there with you, off camera, perhaps, who's holding a gun to your head? Nod slowly, if that's the case and I'll be right round to congratulate him."

Her colleague laughed. One or two tittered round the table.

She had more to say. "Just to recap, then, thirty seconds ago you are dead set against taking him on. I just show you a couple of photos, and suddenly you are all in! Are you joking, just pulling my leg?"

Clicking the photos back to the one that she thought had influenced him, she sensed that he was now staring at his screen situated just below the video-cam he was using.

"Any particular reason at all?" she asked. He never ever admitted to himself that she knew him better than he knew himself. She continued to talk. "Don't you dare think what I think you are thinking. We could get badly burned on this one."

An uncomfortable silence opened up, concern establishing itself unequivocally on her face.
"Look, you are the boss, and if you say 'let's do it', then you know we'll give our heart and soul. I just think this is not us. We've *never* taken this kind of case. And what's more, I have a bad feeling in my bunion."

"Your bunion? Must be all those high shoes you wear."

"Look, what I wear is my business, and I cannot say that you'd even noticed, but I just need to know that we are on the side of the angels here, and I am not sure we are. I show you one photo," she clicked the image to enlarge it, "and, suddenly, you are straining at the leash. Suppose I showed you *this* image?"

He laughed as she showed an image of a baby polar bear.

"Would you still be just as interested?" she asked, raising an eyebrow.

"You know, yes I think I would. I've always loved polar bears!"

Another silence opened and this could only have the effect of increasing her discomfort. "Don't do this to me, I'm getting too old for this."

"Yes, of course Penny. I'm forgetting, and will that be 29 next birthday – so I suppose, that's *really* old! You are serious, aren't you? Surely, it won't be *that* bad"

Once again, her answer came in the form of silence.

She then decided to fill the quiet gap. "Very well, then, as you are so intent on taking this car crash on – I am going to need you in the centre of things."

"I thought we agreed that my skills were best in planning; in the back room?"

"Oh no, not on this one. You are *not* going to get away that lightly. You want it, then, you are going to have to do it, get your hands dirty for once. Besides, in truth, I don't think there's anyone else who could do it, or be foolish enough *to* do it. And I can detect that you want to be involved in this."

"Why do you say that?" he asked, his brow frowning a little.

"Look, you might be a thousand miles away, but I can still read you like a book." At that juncture she knew she had to sit down and did so deflatedly. First she shook her head, but then could not resist the urge to rub her temples. "I will email you the details, project files and the planning files; and then, and only then, assuming you haven't come to your senses, I'll set things in motion. If it's okay with you, I am not going to speak to Lord Bollington just yet, but when we do, I think it should be our 'posh' member who does – and that's you."

"You are just making me pay, because I wanted to take the case on, aren't you?"

"Oh, you are going to pay all right. As soon as this is over we'll all be looking for a pay rise and that holiday to Barbados that you've been promising us now for – five years isn't it?"

Other members nodded and muttered around the table.

"Very well then, it's a deal," he confirmed.

"What! You're agreeing? Oh my god, you really want this, don't you?"

She stared at the picture on the screen. "I just hope it's all worth it and we don't lose our shirt on this."

Switching off the link, she then spoke to the others round the table. "Look, here it is, team, you all heard him; work up the plan as usual. I want an outline strategy within the hour, and then we will add flesh to the bones from there. Get me a list of the resources and personnel we'll need to commit. I should have told him it's going to be expensive, but I suspect even that would not have deterred him."

Her four colleagues went back to their departments and the display panel from the video link ticked as it cooled. She remained in the conference room, looking at the old waterways of Salford Quays. "I just have a bad feeling about all of this," she said aloud. The display panel gave out a tiny shimmer of afterglow, but otherwise there was nobody to hear her warning, or see the unabridged concern now etched on her face.

Chapter V

Corporate Raider

Alexis Mayberry was at work, as usual, when she learned of the unusual and worrying events. Maisie, her Finance Director had come rushing in with a piece of paper. She had placed it front of her boss who was eating a salad at her desk. It wasn't like Maisie to get agitated or upset, but Alexis could detect both of these things, on her expression, as she approached.

"It's true," she said. "Someone is buying our shares like this week's bargain at the discount store. Just take a look at the figures. And so much so, the price is up 4 points on the morning. It's not quite nosebleed levels yet, but it is rising steadily."

"Maisie, not so keen on the discount store analogy you have there, but I catch your drift. So, who is purchasing?"

"Now, that is a good question and one that's hard to answer."

"Really? In today's electronic age, I thought we could tell straight away? And what's this about nosebleeds?"

"You naive person, you," Maisie offered, with a fleeting, but affectionate smile. She continued, "Nosebleed as in *really* high!" Her boss smiled and nodded as she grasped the point.

"As far as I can tell, it seems to be a holding company, like a shell, who's been buying. I am afraid, that could mean anyone from the Ontario Teachers' Pension fund to the Investment Fund managers or even our American friends."

"What! I just can't see that little ol' us would be of even passing interest to any of those?"

"That is also a good question, but someone is buying, and buying big."

"We are surely just too small on a national scene, let alone the international one. I can't think we'd be on anyone's radar, let alone some of the big names you've mentioned."

"Well, think again, Alexis, because you are now centre stage. I suspect that, when others pick up on it, you are certainly going to be a busy girl. I have already had the *Financial Times* on the phone asking me if there is anything I'd like to tell them."

"Oh, yes," she smiled mischievously, "I think it'll be the FD they need to speak to."

"No, you don't. No, not me. I'm just a boffin, tied to my desk. I expect it'll be the brains of the outfit they'll want to speak with. The pretty one, the one who's photogenic as well as clever."

"Surely, I don't pay you enough to get compliments like those."

"You certainly don't. I was just hoping to flatter you enough that you'd do the interviews."

"Don't think so, Maisie, I just run the company, with your invaluable help of course, and don't forget, I've seen that handsome hunk who collects you each evening. I can't think his only interest in you is *just* for your brains."

"Mm, better believe it. Besides, who cares exactly what he's interested in! As long as it's *me* he's interested in. Just because you are married to your work, you know, doesn't mean we can all get away without having a life."

"Yes, yes, I know," she sighed good-naturedly. Recognising a conversation in the offing that they'd had several times before, she decided to attempt a pacifying, pre-emptive strike. "I'll do something about it when I've got time."

"You always say that. *How* old are you? Did I hear thirty or ninety-four? Time is now!"

"Yes, and you always say that."

"No, I don't, last time you were twenty-nine when I said it."

"Okay, I'll elope with a hunky cameraman, when they interview me."

"Chance'd be a fine thing; nothing would please me more. You can still come in and do a bit of work, you know, but perhaps you could stop the all-nighters and the weekends?"

"Now then, there aren't many of those."

"Oh, about four a month, I believe – weekends, that is!"

"Okay, enough! You are putting me off my stride here, and my salad, um, is going cold. Find out who has got us in their cross-hairs, that is what's most important, not my love life."

"What love life?"

"How can we find out?" Alexis had to continue with her questions otherwise she knew her Finance Director would persist with more and more uncomfortable ones.

"I asked the chap who phoned from the *Financial Times*, and he suggested that he might have a contact at the SFO," Maisie offered, sensing that she'd embarrassed her, long suffering, boss.

"The Serious Fraud Office! What's it to do with them? How much trouble are we in?"

"Hopefully none, but getting a little advice cannot hurt, now, can it? I'm told they have access to a lot of inside information. I bet we can get someone to speak to you. As an added bonus it will get you out of the office and let me get on with my job," Maisie teased playfully.

Alexis opened her mouth and even raised a noteworthy finger, but ultimately, her words failed because she decided that just taking her director's advice was probably the path of least resistance.

"Very well then, Maisie, see if you can speak to your friend of a friend of a friend and ask if I can go and quiz someone with his ear to the ground or whatever they do over there."

"I think it's a bit like that, only it's a big ear!"
"Very well then, let's see? And it will also get me out from under your feet!" she could not help but adding. "There might even be a hunky cameraman waiting to sweep me off my 'jimmy choos'. I'd better get my hair done."

"Now, *that* would be too much to hope for," she laughed, suddenly engaged by the prospect of her boss being diverted in this way.

A few days later, Alexis waited outside the office of the contact she'd been given at the SFO. Having barely time to assume a seat, he appeared at the office door within seconds, as if he had been eagerly anticipating her arrival.

"Many thanks for agreeing to meet with me, Mr Forsythe." She shook the greying gentleman's hand.

"Please call me Monty, Miss. It's short for Montague and I hate that even more than Forsythe, so I think it best if we stick to Monty, if that meets with your approval?"

She laughed, "Very well, Monty and I'm Alexis, then, in that case."

Alexis estimated the man before her was in his early sixties. He still had a thick head of hair, but greying had obviously begun some time before. He also wore a crumpled suit and adopted something of a bent posture; most likely spending his days at a desk in front of computer.

He looked at the striking young woman, who was not at all what he'd been told to expect. Words failed him just at that juncture, so he motioned to her to follow him into his office. He had anticipated seeing someone very much like himself, someone who spent all her days at work, just as he did. She was much younger than he, had a vivid sparkle in her eyes as she eagerly scanned the chaotic and crowded shelves of his office. Moreover, they were of an intense blue with a darker rim around the circumference that made them even more fascinating. Most vitally, she espoused a 'joie de vivre' that, apparently, even after devoting long hours to work had not leached out of her – yet. He smiled benevolently upon her and did his best to marshal his thoughts into some semblance of a coherent pattern. It was a shame that he'd never had time for relationships, wondering in that moment, if she would commit the same mistakes he had.

"It has come to my attention that there is a purchaser of the shares in my company. I believe it is a substantial buyer and I am not at all sure why a small insignificant company such as mine should be of interest to others."

"Mmm," he smiled as he considered her question, and continued, "Alexis, to the right person, the right buyer, they are all interesting. Though, unfortunately, in this case, my enquiries are strongly hinting at the 'wrong' buyer."

"Why is that, Monty?"

"Well, it also came to our attention last week that your company was in the spotlight. Our preliminary enquiries are pointing to the work of one man or perhaps I should say it's his 'MO', as in all the crime thrillers. This man, Alexandre Ciesciu, is Romanian by birth, but to Russian parents. It is believed they had angered Stalin, himself, and fled what in those days, of course, was the USSR. Young Alexandre, apparently had a very active mind and quickly discovered a knack for business. Starting off with something pretty small, he soon got into his stride and expanded, so that, in the fullness of time this became, in itself, a very large business."

"Can't say I've ever heard of him," she confirmed.

"He's quite a shadowy character. He tends to work through intermediaries, but believe me, he is the one who pulls the strings. Alexandre has a lot of contacts in southern Russia – the rich kind, but not the nice kind, if you catch my meaning."

She nodded.

"His rise on the world stage has been nothing less than meteoric and we suspect that only a small fraction of his activities are above board. The rest of the 'iceberg' shall we say, disguises some very dodgy dealings we are only now beginning to unravel. The bit we do know is that some years ago he bought an American power company, registered in Idaho. This was barely more than a shell. He then inverted the registration by buying an Irish company."

"One that was domiciled in Ireland?" she asked.

"Yes, quite so, my dear," he confirmed, being impressed with the speed with which she'd caught on. "So, you'll be aware that this saved him a fortune in corporation tax."

"Because the rate is so much lower in Eire," she offered, as he continued to nod encouragingly.

"As I am sure you know, lots of firms do this and it isn't breaking any laws. The next step, also not illegal, was to do the 'double Irish'."

"Pardon?"

"Ah yes." He smiled, sensing he would impart new knowledge, something he enjoyed, or was it simply because it intensified the sparkle from those lovely eyes, that now studied him? "The company funds are once more, moved offshore, say to the Cayman Isles, as in Mr Ciesciu's case. The whole thing then becomes a cash generation machine and, as I said, it is in no way illegal. He lives abroad and again, no laws against this… Though he does many of his deals on the London market, he rarely sets foot in the UK. Following the offshore rules means, inevitably, that he pays no tax to the Exchequer. This, too, is not illegal."

"Forgive me, Monty, but why should I be interested in any of this?"

"Absolutely no earthly reason at all, Alexis, my dear," he admitted urbanely, "except that, for some reason, he is interested in you, or your company, or both." Remaining quiet for a few seconds, he wanted some of his words to sink in, so that the young woman could gauge for herself the problems that faced her. He looked directly at her, with fatherly concern to add further impact, doing his best to retain a grave note in his voice, like a solicitor discussing a family will.

"Tell me, have you taken on any large stock or have you perhaps overstretched the company to service a large order? Have you had a larger than usual capital outlay?"
She nodded, suddenly feeling her stomach disappear as if it were heading down in an express lift.

"Then, Alexis, either you, or, perhaps, I should say your company is in very great danger."

Recognising that he'd scared her enough for the moment, he changed tack. He decided to use a little more information to provide this break. "You need to understand a bit more about this man and the way he operates. Forget what you've learned about the corporate raiders of the past, this man has taken things to a new level. His favourite takeovers are distressed companies, ones who have traded badly, or face short-term cash flow difficulties and those that've bid for large contracts and are financially weakened as a result. Then he strikes, usually with a derisory cash offer. He often raids at dawn, begins a deal way before breakfast, it's all over by lunch, and by dinner he is typically one hundred million richer. The interest he's earned, alone, in that day, is enough to buy a football team.

"I should stress that none of this is illegal and you'll have encountered individuals who made their fortune in this way. Once in control they have sacked the board, put in their own people, sold assets off or simply taken the company private for more money than I could count in my sweetest of dreams. Mr Ciesciu's aggressive style means that he often leverages his deals to create more money, by attracting investors into his schemes. This is why we are interested in him, because we believe that much of this has come from less than transparent sources: Icelandic banks, Russian mafia money or Chinese Triads. If one digs just a little below the surface, then one will find dirty funds. He has access to them all and is certainly not afraid to use them to their all-consuming best.

"We've been after him for years, but in truth we have never come even close to laying a glove on him. Just when we are about to strike, we find he's skipped town and, often, all we come across are teams of lawyers who assure us that it's all above board. In the meantime he is on his way to Famagusta or Georgia; anywhere that does not ask too many questions and allows him to claim offshore status. Our plan is to get someone close to him, with the purpose of obtaining detailed information for us. In our absolute wildest dreams we'd like to try to entice him on to UK soil as we feel, only then, perhaps, we might just be in a position to bring him down. I was hoping that you might be that person."

Her bright expression was now modulated by a distressed, incredulous look.

"Me! Look, I'm just a small-time businesswoman. One who wants nothing to do with people like that, someone who just wants to get on with what I do, what I enjoy doing and hopefully am good at."

"Yes, yes, of course, my dear, and why not." He knew that it was imperative that he continue, despite her alarm. "I understand, I really do," he confirmed, with a fatherly edge creeping into his voice now to match the affectionate way he looked upon her. "I'd love to be able to tell you that it's not a personal thing; that it's just about the money. However, this man seeks more than this; it's almost as though he relishes bringing his prey down. For sure he has riches beyond Croesus. We estimate he could live just on the interest of the massive sums flowing through his companies. However, he wants more than this. He wants to dominate; being the type of a man who has trapped a dolphin, and then likes to watch it struggle in the net, purely for his own edification. Subsequently, he moves on to the next victim with money as the pretext."

She recoiled in horror.

"Sorry, my dear, perhaps too graphic an illustration, but you can get an impression of the type of man we are dealing with?"

"Yes, Monty, I get the picture and it seems an ugly one to me, nothing I want to be anywhere near."

"I have to tell you that I think either you or your company, or both, are in considerable danger."

Alexis shook her head in disbelief. She, the quiet person, the person who never rocked the boat. All she did was work, doing stuff that she loved and yet here was someone for some reason who wanted to take it from her. "Look, my company is mine, and is of no interest to anyone else."

He allowed silence to expose the naivety of her words.

"I own most shares and he can't touch them, not if I don't want to sell."

"You are the major shareholder of a FTSE 500 company. You are a quoted company on the London Stock Exchange," he clarified, redundantly. Then he continued, "and believe me, this has not stopped him in the past. In fact, I would say that this is all he needs. He uses rules of the Stock Exchange and laughs as he drives a coach and horses right through them. Many others have said more or less the same thing. They retired a few days later, to a man and a woman, somewhat richer, it has to be said, but someone who was made surplus to the requirements of their own company."

"I'm not interested in having anything to do with him."

"Sadly, that option is no longer available to you."

"I am not the person you need here. I am just going to do what I do best, and hopefully he will grow bored and move on to some other unsuspecting business."

"I doubt that. I suspect your only way forward is to join forces with us and let's find out if we can bring him down."

"I am just not interested."

"Very well, I can see when a deal is a non-starter." He knew he'd gone as far as he dared. Perhaps he'd shocked her too much, overworked the deal, maybe. In any event the poor girl was terrified. He realised all he could do now was to allow her some space to think and hope that she might come back to him.

"Thank you for your time, Miss. Please forgive me if I look disappointed. You were the first real chance we've had of getting anywhere near him for years. I was hoping that you'd be the one: the one with the silver bullet, to rid us of this evil."

"Sorry, I'm not that girl," she looked away in that moment, acutely aware of mutual discomfort, but tinged more with fear on her part. "May I go?"

"Yes, yes, of course, my dear," he stood up just as she did, "but of course." He managed a weak smile.

Pausing momentarily, she looked down, allowing the vivid blue dress to assume its correct height of just above the knee. The shapely, pale legs sported spiky shoes in a 'nude' colour, which had the cachet of being eternally fashionable as well as flattering to most girls' legs.

He shook her hand, his grip being both a little too warm and too moist for her liking, as he returned the anaemic smile. "I'm sure that you won't change your mind, but if I may? Here is my card and, it goes without saying that I shall be at your service night or day."

The smile flickered, but only for an instant. Long fingers retained the little card, which he'd offered, but then thought no more about.

Leaving his offices a short time later, she retrieved her red Range Rover Evoque in a nearby car park. Driving out of London, she selected her favourite music in an attempt to distract herself from unhappy thoughts that washed over her like an oil slick on a previously pristine sandy beach. She continued travelling west, bound for her home in Kingston-upon-Thames.

Darkness was in the ascendant as she parked on her drive, too distracted to contemplate navigating the garage, despite the frosty evening. Fumbling in the pitch black for her front door keys, she wandered in absent-mindedly and deactivated the alarm system, her thoughts still on other things. Putting on more lights than one person needed, she attempted to banish the gathering night. Although she had always lived alone, she had never felt lonely until, for some reason, tonight. Taking up position in her kitchen, with the bright illumination and gleaming surfaces, she sat with a cup of tea, unable to comprehend the nature of the vacuum that had opened in the middle of her life.

She had always worked; work was her life. Perhaps Mr Forsythe had simply reminded her of this, or perhaps something more. He had reminded her that any businessperson's life may be, professionally speaking, a fleeting one. Only in the small hours of the morning did she finally grasp the central tenet, which caused her most uneasiness – that there was no one with whom she could share her unsettling private thoughts.

A poor night's sleep awaited. Finding herself pacing the floor of the large, but empty house, she resorted to flicking 'on' the telly and putting on some music. Sadly, neither of these strategies achieved any success. Even reading the *Companies' Directory*, which usually never failed to induce a deep sleep, was a wasted and boring exercise. At 3am, she began hunting round, looking for the card that she'd been given and retained – somewhere. Ultimately, it was only by braving the cold and going out to her car, in her thin nightclothes and fluffy slippers, that she discovered the elusive card, having left it on the front seat. From the chaos, some conclusions came to her at this juncture and having done so, were accompanied by a calmer, more settled frame of mind. She was able to sleep a short time later.

Rising early, she sat fully dressed at the long white worktop that divided her kitchen. The roof lights allowed the first ingress of a new spring day. She activated the large, but vanishingly thin TV, on her wall. Selecting the Financial Channel, she sat there with a sense of anticipation. Inevitably, she wasn't unduly surprised to see the name of Mr Ciesciu appear within a few minutes. Graphs displayed the performance of his latest acquisition, a speciality steel coating and finishing business thought to be have been worth half a billion pounds in happier times. Following an aggressive and spectacular raid, he'd bought it for one hundred million pounds sterling.

Suddenly, thoughts were translated into actions. Tapping the phone on the wall next to her, she dialled Mr Forsythe's number. Only then did she look at the clock. It was just after 6am. Reasoning with only a little guilt that he'd assured her that any time would be convenient for him, she pressed on with the call. She could only assume that he was in earnest. True to his word, Mr Forsythe answered the phone with neither delay nor the sleepy overtones of someone who'd just had their sleep interrupted. In fact he seemed to be not only wide-awake, but also nothing short of delighted to hear from her so soon, as if he'd been waiting all night in the hope that she might just contact him.

"Very well, then, Mr Forsythe, ah Monty. Secret agent Alexis, here, reporting for duty. Is it okay to still answer to this name, or are you going to have to assign me an alias, after the plastic surgery to alter my appearance, of course."

"No, no, Miss Alexis, it would be a travesty to alter in any way those delightful looks of yours."

"Why thank you, Monty," she offered, with more embarrassment creeping into her voice than she would have liked, thereby revealing that compliments were a stranger to her lonely life.

Mercifully, the older man took up the thread of the conversation without delay, thus sparing her the pause that would otherwise have caused discomfiture. "Are you able to meet with me and a colleague at any time today, any time and place of your convenience, Miss Alexis?"

Later that morning, Mr Forsythe appeared at her offices in the Strand still wearing the same clothes that he had on the day before, thus lending support to her view that he'd indeed been waiting by the phone all night. He introduced a younger colleague, a petite mousey woman, with small but bright eyes. He referred to as Miss McCready.

Alexis was expecting a thick paper-based file, a dusty dossier of information perhaps, but was pleasantly surprised when he handed over a slim 10-inch tablet device.

"I hope you don't mind Miss, Miss, Alexis." She nodded slowly as the words were formed a little uneasily on his lips. The younger colleague smiled a little as he did so. "I have loaded all the relevant files on this tablet. It contains all the information we have and, in addition, relevant links to search engines, and so on, to spare you time. I also feel it prudent to ask you not to approach Mr Ciesciu directly as we feel it simply too dangerous. The information we have gathered on the tablet is for a man called Toby Richmond. He is a close colleague of our Russian friend. Few deals are done without him being made aware. We would be very pleased to interview him as an important, but low hanging fruit, manoeuvre, if you follow, uh Alexis."

She nodded, not wanting to interrupt the words that were now flowing with more nervousness on his part than she'd noted the day before.

"He is not such an unsavoury character as Mr Ciesciu, but he does have widespread knowledge that we can use to plot a way forward. Trouble is that he operates under the offshore rules, also, and usually spends little time in the UK. On the table you will find his whereabouts and his interests, the places he frequents and, in addition, his leisure pursuits. Tell me Alexis," he asked as he finally relaxed, "do you ski?"

"As a matter of fact, yes, and I even got to the black ski-league, but I haven't skied for years. When I was 18, I spent the whole winter skiing on the east coast of Canada and then as the snow failed I was able to go to the west coast and finish the season in Whistler."

"That's perfect then, as this man is an avid skier and we have suggested one or two scenarios where you might be able to bump into him, accidentally on purpose. We are of the view that an acute-minded person such as yourself will be able to glean important information not only about the interest they have in your company, but many other deals as well. I don't know if you'll be able to tempt him to London or the UK, but this would give us the opportunity to interview him directly. I should emphasise that this is a way in for us and any information will help us. Once we have gained some intelligence, shall I say, in this way, we hope to be able to help you. One other word of warning, he is a gentleman, or perhaps, I should say male, who should be regarded as unsafe in taxis."

"Forgive me Monty, what does 'unsafe in taxis' mean?" Alexis just had to ask. Miss McCready was also looking very puzzled, as she looked at him.

"Ah, yes apologies, it was in widespread use when I was your age, and refers to no young lady wanting to be alone in a taxi with such a person. Perhaps, these days, you younger ones might use 'a bit of a lady-killer'?"

Alexis wasn't entirely sure that even this was still in common usage, but at least she understood that he meant 'player' and she smiled at the old-world charm of the senior gentleman who perhaps didn't get out much.

"Well, Monty, I am a businesswoman and, as you know, my aim is to protect my business, something that I care passionately about. I doubt whether some lecherous ladies' man will deflect or distract me – taxi or no taxi," she declared, not quite able to diminish the dazzling smile, as she did so.

"Yes, of course, quite so my dear," he agreed, as even his grey hair appeared to blush.

She continued. "I don't think his charms will work on me, and I believe that I will enjoy bringing him, and his unsavoury associates, down."

"Ah, yes, we were hoping that you might say that," he returned with some delight as he looked at his colleague.

"I should say, that we are contactable at any time. Furthermore, we will do our best to be within support distance, should you need us. Feel free to phone or text or email at any time; the relevant details and the appropriate links are on the tablet, but please enter them, also, on your personal phone. We will, unfailingly, be at your service 24 hours a day, seven days a week."

"You mean 24/7?"

"Yes, quite so, my dear," he laughed.

"Oh, another important thing. We retain responsibility for all your expenses, howsoever incurred. Here is a special credit card that allows for an unlimited amount and is universally accepted. It also has a cash withdrawal limit of ten thousand pounds per day." Across the desk he slid a black credit card with characters that were raised in a relief that looked like pure molybdenum. Looking with sheer fascination at the card, as it shone in the overhead lighting, just in front of her, she noticed that her name was embossed on it.

"If you'd be good enough to sign the strip on the back, whilst I am here, then I can leave it with you. The PIN is the year that you graduated with your MBA at Harvard."

"I am very impressed by how much you seem to know about me, Mr Forsythe. The thing that perturbs me, is that I wonder if you've had these things in place for some days."

He read her thought instantly.

"Please do not be offended, Miss." He looked at the shining black card he'd placed on her desk, for that moment, not quite able to maintain eye contact. "They could always be cancelled more quickly than they could be put in place."

"Yes, I'm sure that's true." If a nuance of concern and irritation crossed her face, it was gone by the time her intense blue eyes and radiant smile were offered in his direction, causing his arthritic knees to tremble just a little.

"Ah yes, well, it only remains for me to wish you luck and of course we will be eagerly monitoring your progress. Many thanks for helping us with this matter."

Her two visitors rose at this point, both shaking her hand as she also stood.

As soon as they had vacated her offices, she sat up straight behind her glass pedestal desk and turned on the tablet. It flared into life immediately with a brilliant, vivid colour that lit up her face and room. Insatiable curiosity flowed as soon as she opened the first file. The picture of the man she was to intercept appeared, occupying the whole screen.

"Hello, handsome and what a looker you are! Lady-killer or not, that won't save you. If it's you or my company, you're as good as done for. One of us going down in flames, for sure."

Chapter VI

Fates Locked as One

The following day, Alexis took the first flight out of London City Airport bound for Innsbruck, where, upon arrival, a private taxi awaited her.

A short time later she was checking in at her hotel in Mayrhofen, Austria. She looked up at the lifts conveying thousands of skiers to the slopes. Accepting that it had been many years since she'd been on skis, she was eagerly anticipating reacquainting herself with a sport that at one time had brought her much enjoyment. There was a party atmosphere in the village, and smiling to herself, she glanced at the excited faces of those waiting for the lifts.

Without waiting to unpack, she simply retrieved her newly acquired ski jacket, old boots and salopettes and headed to the ski-hire shop. She looked at her antiquated ski boots that had seen better days and were also of an obsolete design. Imbibing something of the energy and elation within the outfitters, she saw row upon row of the latest ski equipment. Deciding in that moment to treat herself to new gear, she looked with amazement at the blacker-than-black credit card, which gleamed like obsidian in the shop's spotlights. She realised, that although it would be perfectly acceptable for her to settle this and every other bill using the card, ultimately the not inconsequential funds behind it must come from the public purse. Feeling guilty, she decided to pay for the new kit herself.

An hour later she left the outfitters sporting a pair of the latest, expertly fitted ski boots, complete with moulded insoles and heat-bonded clamshell casings. She hired a pair of the latest skis, and with a little thrill, she confirmed to the attendant that she was an expert skier. He'd set the settings on the ski-bindings accordingly. Her white helmet had a rose-tinted integrated visor, which simply hinged down to protect one's face and eyes.

As the excitement mounted within her, it stirred long dormant memories of the passion she'd held for skiing and friends she'd encountered in what now seemed like a previous life. A life that had been put on hold after her mum had died and she'd started her business. She realised, in a seminal moment that she'd been subsumed totally by this life she had created. Consequently the young person had been replaced undeniably by a businesswoman. Shaking her head, she rejected such unhappy and wayward thoughts. She loved her business, loved it more than anything – surely, everyone knew that.

Wafting her left hand with the ski-pass card in the vague direction of the security barrier, she passed through as the indicator glowed green. Then she moved on to the small queue for the cable car, which whisked people up to the slopes with typical Austrian engineering efficiency. Her phone went off just as she got into the bubble, almost forgetting to place her skis in the rack outside the car and to take her poles inside with her.

"Hello Miss, it's Carrie, here. I am a colleague of Mr Forsythe. Please head straight up and we believe your target is at the top of the black run."

Gulping nervously, she knew the black runs in the resort could be challenging and would normally not pose a problem for her.

However, having not been on skis for over ten years did not fill her with confidence. Supposedly one never forgot how to ski: once learned it was like riding a bicycle. She had a feeling that she was going to test this theory fairly soon.
"Good luck, Miss Alexis, we'll text you later," Carrie offered, and the call was terminated.

Sitting back in the télécabine, she was conveyed at speed up to the top of a very steep mountain. She saw the sun appear over snow-covered peaks, the cloud layer appearing as an inversion now below her. There it was: seemingly the roof of the world and surely the seat of Creation itself. She breathed in deeply, having forgotten the dizzy vitality of pure mountain air. How could she have neglected all this, and so much more that she might discover in the days ahead?

Another four-man lift took her to the top of the deserted black run. She checked the ski bindings, which looked secure, and adjusted the clasps on her boots. Upon considering the steep slope ranged in front of her she looked down with dismay. It appeared much steeper than her memories told her she was used to and the cold air had turned it to ice. To make matters worse, the surface had then been broken presumably by a temporary thaw in the night which had the effect of breaking up or 'crazing' the surface into small discs of ice – the so-called 'death cookies' that every skier hated.

This essential attribute of every modern-day carving ski was the radius of the curve, inbuilt along the sides. Ultimately, however, it was the blade-like border of the ski that allowed the skier to descend steep, icy gradients in safety, but at speed. The curve allowed a turn to be made simply by applying the edge: tilting or 'carving' the downhill ski, which would then describe a curve according to its radius. Weight would be applied to the downhill ski until such time as a turn was needed, whereupon, the uphill one would be readied going into the turn, to take over. As each turn was completed, this ski would then become the downhill one. Using such means, the skier was able to link turns together and thus descend some very steep slopes.

From the photos on her tablet, she recognised her target, Toby Richmond, coming off another lift on the south side of the ski area. Recalling events later, she would never know what made her set off when she did and in the way she did. She could only think that it was nerves and a sense of urgency that caused the subsequent events.

Taking off precipitously with neither a strategy nor consideration of the black run was to prove catastrophic for Alexis, because she lost control from the outset. The smooth slippery surface provided very little purchase, even for a well-positioned ski, and could offer only extreme danger to the unwary skier who had set off in such a manner.

The skis whipped up speed very quickly. Her direction across the fall line of the gradient seemed, initially, perfectly appropriate. Unfortunately, she allowed her skis to remain flat so that their entire, waxed and polished, surface was in contact with the steep and unforgiving slope. Only the razor *edge* of the ski could have either slowed her or turned her, but because of her poorly balanced start, this was not on offer. Before she could even gasp, the speed accelerated to levels that had she acted immediately, would have been hard to control.

She was about to encounter a velocity well over that expected for safe passage down the run. Sadly, loss of control went hand-in-hand with unrestrained speed. Furthermore, her pathway down the mountain took her across the slope and therefore to its edge where a precipitous and rocky drop awaited her. As the milliseconds passed, her swift and unstructured descent was limiting her options, her time to think and, most vitally, time to act – even if she were able to. Total panic set in at this point. Waving her arms in desperation, she then did something purely by reflex making the situation worse. She leaned back in her bindings. Even novice skiers were taught never to do this, for it placed more weight on the rear of the skis forcing the front tips to rise upwards, thus reducing control even further.

Toby came off the four-man lift and saw Alexis rush by. Recognising the danger she was in, he willed her to put a turn in, and soon, or she'd be off the edge of the piste and, without doubt, the mountain. Moreover, he was aware that at the rate and angle she was travelling, it was extremely unlikely that the safety netting would restrain her. He shuddered, thinking that there was every possibility that she would transect the barriers and hurtle to a cold and violent death on the outcrops below.

Perhaps it was fortunate that he couldn't allow himself the luxury of further thought or planning – time was too scarce. Setting off straightaway, he pushed his poles viciously on the unforgiving surface to set himself in motion. He quickly assumed a very low tuck position to reduce wind resistance. Despite feeling the rush of air biting his face at the edges of his ski goggles and the wind howling past his ears, he knew he needed still more speed. He tucked in even lower.

Mercifully, his weight and height dictated that he be fitted with longer and therefore more efficient skis, conferring a slight advantage. Due to this, his descent acceleration was faster than hers. Agonisingly, he gained on her. The ice under the skis made a horrible scraping noise, denoting the difficulty of retaining control. Even expert skiers would devote every effort to limit their speed to raise the margin of safety; he was doing his utmost, to do the opposite. Continuing to plot the very same course as she, he followed her path that would, if not corrected, lead to certain extinction.

He could see that she was trying to form a snow-plough in an attempt to slow down. This was a manoeuvre practised by beginners where skis are brought to an 'A' shape – the outer edges then angled upwards enabling the ski edges to cut into the surface, and so destroy acceleration. Unhappily, not only was Alexis was going too fast for this to have any impact, but even the strongest legs would be unable to maintain such a configuration on this glacial and sheer terrain. Furthermore, in making the attempt she wasted more of the rapidly diminishing time still available to her.

Her move was destined to fail before she had begun it – doomed, like her. Toby willed the female skier to turn, her only hope; for, stopping had long since become impossible. The wind continued to howl at them both as the brutal, precipitous edge beckoned.

At least she'd moved her weight forward a little over the skis and this would provide some assistance for the daring manoeuvre he was contemplating. Logic dictated that if she couldn't turn, then he was going to have to turn for her – such a strategy remained solely within the gift of time itself. Oblivion called to them in that moment: it could be heard in the rush of the skis over the ice, and felt via the lacerating wind that cut his face. The whole mountain appeared to roar as it prepared to claim its prize of two unwary and foolish souls.

The edge of the piste could clearly be seen a short distance away, and would be reached in less time than one needed to draw a couple of breaths. Inevitably, there was no time left, even for a prayer. Only he was moving faster than anything else, save for the wind, on that cruel mountain: racing either to rescue her or to ski off the mountain with her – no other outcome was in the offing now. Wondering in that moment if he'd acted too late, too foolishly or too hastily, he was about to couple his fate with hers. He realised, just before the edge readied to dash them, that given the choice and sufficient time, he would do the same again. Under no circumstances could he have stood back and watched.

The precious, but fleeting moment at hand, he made a desperate lunge for Alexis. In presenting the flat face of his own skis to the ice, his heavier weight, longer skis and unremitting determination to catch her had won for him what might only be a short-lived gain, before a Pyrrhic victory claimed them both. He spread his skis as far apart as he dared.

His legs widened to such an extent that they were able, barely, to pass either side of both of hers and encompass them within their span. Reaching for her, he placed his hands around her slim waist. He locked them in front of her, their fate now declared jointly as one entity. They hurtled across the slope, the edge of the piste just metres away. The time in which they'd cover such distance could, with certainty, be measured in heartbeats. Bringing himself up to his full height, he was going to need some flexion from both his knees – imminently – if he were to stand a chance of saving them both. With prodigious effort, his legs closed together, summoning strength that only fear of impending disaster could provide; his height came up. Only then could he even consider a turn.

They flashed past the piste markers. A light dusting of snow could be found at this edge, well beyond the area that skiers would contemplate. The noise of the skis' transit changed as they encountered this thin coating: the flimsy crash barrier danced with uncertainty before them. He felt, rather than heard, her scream, so closely were they entwined. Holding her a little more tightly, he knew, at the very least, she was not about to die alone. Inevitably their speed continued to accelerate.

By approximating his legs together, his skis had also straightened hers as they swept them both parallel: all four in contact, for the first time. He was ready to begin the turn. Slightly spinning her torso towards the left, he pulled at her waist. His shoulder came up as he offloaded his weight from both his skis - this being the only way to make them change direction. The skiers stared straight down the fall line and the gaping maw of the drop that awaited came into clear view. She screamed again, now purely at the mercy of death itself, which felt no need for hurry. Closing her eyes, because all she could see was a cataclysm of horror.

He wanted to shout back, above the roar of the wind, that he would save her or die alongside her in the attempt, but all his efforts, strength and concentration were directed to the turn that must come – and soon.

It was always said that those who faced impending and violent deaths would see their lives flash before them. She, however, saw, in that scintilla of time passing remorselessly, the young life that had barely begun, one that contained so little – almost as if its inconsequential nature meant it would hardly be missed.

He held her still more tightly. He positioned his cheek against the back of her shoulder, frantically trying to look the way they must go rather than where they were headed. Only at that point could he attempt to put pressure on to the right ski – if he could *just* get it to turn. All his weight and all his strength was then applied to its inner edge, forcing the curved blade into the ice, which protested with an even more thunderous scraping noise. All at once, the sharp edge began to bite. The radius of the turn was fixed, if he were able to hold it, himself and her. At first the ski refused to sustain their collective weight at such a speed, on so steep a gradient, and on such ice, for it started skidding – marking their death throes rhythmically as it flapped up and down. The crash netting loomed within inches, the restraining poles at awkward angles, which meant they would pop out on the slightest contact, and for sure, with the impact that was about to test them to destruction.

He placed more weight to the right ski, dipping his shoulder as he summoned everything in his legs, his core – all was committed now to a ski edge a few microns thick. He remembered a trick that an instructor had taught him, when attempting a tight manoeuvre – press the big toe down within the boot as far as one was able. This increased the pressure on the downhill ski that he was begging to turn. The gap between life and death now hovered precariously on the edge of a single ski. Agonisingly the ski bit and, therefore, even at that speed, began to change direction; unfortunately, by nowhere near enough. Despite his worthy efforts, insufficient space remained for them to deny death. As a teenager, his ski instructor had implored him to 'wait for the ski to turn'. He knew that it would complete this long after they were both off the cliff.

Having one last desperate move, he rotated his knee inwards so that the downhill ski, now bearing their entire weight, was deliberately angled almost perpendicular to the fall line. This so-called 'stem out' turn effectively moved them further along the arc that the ski described. His right leg punished him with severe pain – but the ski responded. Ultimately it meant safety, for it moved them away from that precipice, which whisked by as he clung to her. One tiny, but vital, fact also applied, without which all of his efforts would have been in vain – his legs were longer than hers. This allowed him to encompass both of her skis, even when set in an angled snowplough, within his. Continuing to squeeze round her waist, in that moment, terrified of letting her go, he saw the edge of the cliff barely a metre away. He could feel her sharp intake of air, a gulp of unadulterated fear, while she wondered if she'd just taken her last breath.

The stem turn had, however, ensured that their trajectory was now back towards the main piste. Exhaling with almost hysterical relief, it seemed he had not breathed for the entire manoeuvre; she felt his hot breath on her cheek. Though finally heading for safety, he moved his left leg to run parallel with the right that had completed the stem turn. Her skis were sweeping with his so that all four, once again, ran together side by side. In order to check the speed, the easiest way for the exhausted skier was to head back across the piste and then put in a slight upturn so that gravity would now aid them rather than bring about their destruction. He held her for a vital few moments longer, neither party daring to believe that their ordeal was over, nor that their escape from an unpleasant death had been so close.

They came to rest on the left side of the piste. Only at that point did he let go of her, pushing her gently forwards so that he could disengage his own skis. He then passed on her right hand side, downhill of her, so that she could not slip below him.

Her first instinct was to sob and to weep at her deliverance. Abject embarrassment, however, stepped in and dictated a very different approach.

"Wow! Nice moves," she offered with more confidence than her stampeding heart, shaking legs and quivering voice could support. She placed her poles in the hard icy surface with some effort and lifted the visor off her face to allow her to see her saviour.

"Are you all right? Forgive me for manhandling you in that way, when we haven't been introduced."

"Look, next time I am heading down the quick way, you can manhandle me all you want.

I am sorry to have put you at such risk. I cannot thank you enough."

Lifting his own goggles, she was surprised when she saw him up close, for his pictures did not do him justice. The deep, steady and honest eyes surveyed her with concern.

"I'm Toby."

She pulled off a ski glove on her right hand to engage with the one he'd offered, "Alexis, and I am *very* pleased to meet you. I'd have *definitely* been over the edge if it hadn't been for you." She didn't dare look back at the way they'd come, her rampaging heart and pulsating brain both counselled against such an attempt.

He offered, "Quite possibly," deciding to keep to himself, the thought 'most definitely'. "Tell me, had you strayed on to the wrong slope?"

There it was, that amazing smile aimed full on, straight at her as she blinked somewhat nervously towards him; the morning light was coming in at an angle as it illuminated her pert nose and well-formed cheekbones.

"No, I just should've started with something gentler."

"Started!"

"Sorry, no, I meant to say that this is the first time back on skis for ten years. I used to be, or thought I was, a good skier."

The full smile engaged with hers, once again, as the bright day added its blessing.

"Ten, years! That explains it," answering his own question. "I can't wait for the season to start. I'm usually on the first lift up."

"Yes, I can believe that, and in any event I am pleased you were on this slope today. Come on, can I at least buy you a drink?"

"Are you okay to…" he began, meaning to ask her if she was confident to ski down the icy black run that had nearly claimed them both. However, as he looked back at her, she had already performed a slick 180-degree turn so as to head back onto the piste and down the steep run. Moreover, her linked turns were a thing of beauty. The skis were held parallel and very close together, a position that the experts invariably adopted. Her movements metronomically flowing from one turn to the next. Skiing behind her, he discovered a confident skier that would impress even a seasoned aficionado.

Minutes later, they reached the mountain restaurant. After locating their skis in the rack outside, they went inside.

"Well, I can see that you have got your ski legs back."

"Yes, I am so sorry. I feel very foolish."

"Don't give it a second thought, I was thinking the day could have done with some excitement."

"Now, that I don't believe."

He laughed. "Perhaps a little too much excitement? So, Alexis what has caused you to return to skiing after a ten-year break?"

"Well, I spent much of my gap year skiing in Canada. Then my Mum died and it was time to get serious, hence the long time frame. I suppose I buried myself in my work."

"I'm sorry to hear about your Mum."

"That's okay, it's now a long time ago. So, how about you, what brings you to Austria?"

"I spend much of the season in the Alps, the Dolomites, wherever the snow is good. This is my favourite area, however. When I get fed up, or the snow fails, then, I fly south to the sun to Paphos, or Dubrovnik to catch a little warmth."

"So, do you work?" she asked, her curiosity increasing with the replies he gave.

"Oh, yes, indeed I do, but I tend to move from project to project and I am brought in, shall I say, when my colleagues feel that I'm needed. We're intensively busy for a while, then there's a bit of a break, and it's time to do some more skiing or some sailing, or hopefully both!"

"Wow, that's wonderful. Anything you are working on at the moment?"

He smiled. "Oh, always looking for suitable opportunities. So, what line of work are you in?"

"Nothing much, it sounds pretty boring in comparison with what you do. I run a small company. I doubt you'll have heard of it."

Just at this point his dessert was brought to the table. She looked at it suspiciously. The whole thing looked like an igloo and it reminded her of heaps of suet dumplings that she'd been required to eat at school. It certainly didn't look any more appetising. Its only saving grace was that the whole thing had been doused in vanilla custard, which, at least, gave off a tantalising smell.

Sensing her antipathy towards one of his favourite puddings, he began, "Go on, have a go? Share it with me? It's too much for one person to eat," he lied.
Somewhat hesitantly she took her fork and stabbed at it. Being surprised when the plum filling oozed out and with just a little less reluctance, she raised it to her lips, doing her best not to sniff at it, as might a dog searching for narcotics. Gamely, she slipped it carefully inside her mouth, the pink lips flushing, almost imperceptibly, as the hot pudding entered.

"Wow! That's amazing," she said, now pointing to it as one might at a magician who'd just teleported himself across a crowded stage.

"Thought you'd like that," he confirmed, the delight running on his every feature. "It's called a *germknödel*, an Austrian speciality."

They continued to share the pudding, and she found herself eating with more passion as the wonderful flavours appeared with each mouthful. He took steadily smaller chunks of it and insisted that she finish off the last and tastiest portion, patting his stomach as if he could eat no more. Her enthusiasm, for a moment, did not register his polite restraint. His delight in seeing her eat with such vigour outweighed his hunger.

What a puzzle this man was. Without doubt, he was not what she'd been expecting. Whenever she looked up, there was that steady open expression and those intense yet revealing eyes that seemed totally focussed on her and to the exclusion of all else. Though she'd had limited experience with men. She remembered her last date, now over two years ago, who'd spent the evening looking at every tense cleavage and high hemline that came through the door. She felt quietly disappointed that he was such a bad guy, as there was much to admire and like.

Motioning for the bill, Toby insisted that it was his treat. Then he shot to his feet, so much so that she gave a little start.

"Come on, let's do some more skiing."

He knew the slopes so well. Never having been to this area before, she was content to tag along. At first he watched her carefully, but then, on seeing that her confidence was fully restored, he was happy either to ski at her side, where the slope permitted, or behind her where narrowness of the piste required it.

All too soon, the sun faded from the sky and visibility levels started falling. It was to be their last run of the day. Crossing a snow-covered ridge, they found their way down to the village.

A member of the ski patrol approached. "I'm sorry, there's an avalanche warning in force; the warm conditions have created an unstable zone ahead of you. We are closing this area with immediate effect. I'm afraid you'll have to ski back the way you came, or back to the télépherique."

Toby knew that this would mean retracing their steps by some miles. Turning to Alexis he said, "My chalet is just over that ridge back there. Do you fancy living a little more dangerously?"

She thought quickly. Here it was, 'unsafe in taxis' as Mr Forsythe had put it. She wondered with a smile if he also meant 'unsafe in mountain chalets'. No doubt she would be charmed with food and wine and then promptly seduced before the morning light graced her with its presence. Something of his nature, his friendliness, and yes, his charm, combined with the glorious mountain air. Furthermore, the fact that she'd been given a break from her steady unchanging work routines meant that the answer appeared before she could allow caution to overcome it.

"Yes, why not. How much extra danger can I be in for one day?"

"Shall we find out?" He offered with the winning smile that visited his face so readily.

He led the way. They climbed a little, which required more exertion than she could cope with as tiredness supervened, until, finally, she unclipped her skis and walked up the hill. He took off his own skis at that juncture to help her. Upon reaching the top of the ridge, they were then able to ski down into the adjacent valley.

There, nestling halfway to the valley floor was the most wonderful chalet she had ever seen. Built in the traditional Austrian style, the wood was still pale, which meant that it had probably been recently completed. There was a veranda facing down the slope of the valley that appeared to run around three of the external walls. She saw the Ski-doo, snowmobile, parked outside, which answered her question as to how one would get in with one's luggage and out for supplies, this far from the village.

One entire wall contained double-height glass windows. As they approached, she could see the beautifully turned wooden spindles that made up the balusters of the balcony. In addition, the outside log store, for the wood burner, which was protected by a porch, led to an underground boot and ski store, complete with electrically-heated boot rails. She followed him down into the cellar. Easing out of her new boots, she slipped them on the heated loops, which would retain them until needed and ensure that upon her return they would be toasty warm, and perfectly dry.

"Hopefully the runs will be open by morning, but in the meantime you're stuck with me, I'm afraid."

Reflecting that this was not a bad place to be, she could, without doubt, think of worse people to be stuck with. Wondering when he would display his lady killer credentials, she smiled with more curiosity and fascination than disapproval.

"I'm sure I'll cope, somehow," she confirmed. The glorious mountain air had something of a giddy influence upon her.

"Fancy a drink? What would you like? Hot, cold, soft or hard?"

"Go on, surprise me," she offered, suddenly feeling more carefree than she had in a long time.

Watching while he made her a 'Balibu', coffee with Malibu and Baileys, she took the drink from him with almost a sense of adventure, never having had one before. There was something about holidays, and skiing in particular, which worked a magical effect on food in general, and alcoholic drinks in particular. They sat in the main room and he stirred the log fire back to life. She noted the double-height, wood panelled ceiling and the staircase with gallery rail that presumably led to the bedrooms.

Looking through the far wall, which was glazed to the whole height of the room, she caught the glorious colours of the sunset as it withdrew its influence over the mountains, ready for the night to descend.

"Bit of bad news, I'm afraid I am not a very good cook. Pizza deliveries can take an age up here, especially with the delivery drivers tending to get eaten by hungry polar bears."

She laughed.

"However, this is a personal favourite of mine. They tell me, it's not half bad."

She continued to sip her drink. He then offered her a glass of chilled white wine while she watched him cook.

"This is wonderful, Toby. What a great life you have."

"Oh, it's not mine. I just borrow it from a friend."

"Your life or the chalet?" she asked mischievously.

"Oh, both!" he confirmed.

"What super friends you have!" She pointed to a framed picture sitting on a wooden shelf above the fire. It was a picture of an older man, a woman next to him with two small children. "Is that, your friend's family?"

"Yes, yes indeed it is."

Alexis remembered at that point how skiing in the mountains would always induce hunger and was grateful when he offered her a small cast-iron pan served on a wooden mat. The whole thing looked like a mix of an omelette and a classic English breakfast. They ate enthusiastically and she nodded appreciatively at the food she'd been given.

"Is this another Austrian speciality?"

"Yes indeed, and another favourite of mine. It's called a 'Tiroler Gröstl', and I think basically it means 'fry up'."

He offered her a glass of wine, and then another. The evening passed quickly and enjoyably. She was surprised that despite being the epitome of friendship, he'd made no move to seduce her. Keeping a respectful distance, he was warm, almost affectionate, and looked at her with interest and appreciation rather than trying to picture her without her clothes. The more she studied him, his bright friendly manner and his willingness to engage in conversation, the more puzzled she became.

Eventually, she stood up and asked him if she could turn in. He got up quickly, sensing that she was more tired than he'd guessed and showed her to her room. He also found her an oversized T-shirt and a new toothbrush. After showering, she got into the comfortable bed. Just before sleep claimed her, she was aware of him showering and then finding his own bed. A smile came to her as she entered her sleep slope, the second occasion that had happened in the past week.

She awoke the following day to realise that the exercise, the mountain air and the wholesome food, together with the drinks, had all combined to create a deep and peaceful sleep. One that she'd not enjoyed for many years. At home she would always have things on her mind, worries about her business, stock levels and orders. Inevitably, her thoughts would progress as she'd wonder whether to spend more time and, or money to overextend both herself and the business to strive for greater profits.

Sometime in the night, however, another event intruded upon her. She became aware of an intense white light coming in through her window and with it an unfamiliar reverberating mechanical noise. In the hypnogogic state that existed between sleep and wakefulness, this initially terrified her. The incandescent light began moving along the walls, even piercing the blinds that she'd drawn. Thinking that the source must be pretty close, for the whole chalet seemed to be shaking. At first she wondered if an alien spacecraft had just landed next to them, or if the chalet had suddenly departed its foundations and was about to slip down the mountain. Only then did she realise that it was a piste-basher preparing the runs for the following day. Recognition brought with it both calmness and reassurance. The massive machine went about its dogged work with the pulsating noise that resonated all around, across the mountain, and now, seemingly, through her.

Chapter VII

Ghostly Apparition

Alexis and Toby awoke to find pristine slopes, courtesy of the work of the piste-bashers and also a heavy 'dump' as the skiers liked to refer to it, of fresh snow. They did not waste their morning, as sunshine and skiing were an invigorating mix. The conditions on the runs were also much better than the day before. Each descent could be attempted with even more enjoyment as the carving skis, when handled well, proved thrilling and exhilarating.

Finding another mountain restaurant at lunchtime, he introduced her to another of his local favourites, *kaiserschmarm*, and, once again, he took delight in her looking uncertainly at the pudding at first, before eating it with excitement.

After lunch Toby informed her that he was travelling west to the balloon festival that evening. For a fleeting moment she seemed disappointed that he would be leaving her and hoped that such emotion would not appear on her bright expression.

"Of course, you'd be welcome to come with me, if balloon festivals are your thing?"

She wasn't sure what a balloon festival was, but she successfully withheld curiosity and delight from her countenance. She managed to delay words for long enough for him to think it was a regular, almost routine, thing for her to do. "Oh, go on then, I'll accompany you if you'd like. I was only going to have an evening meal in the hotel."

"Very well then, I'll pick you up in a couple of hours, if that would be convenient? Wear your ski gear though. It gets cold waiting for the balloons to appear."

At the appointed hour, a silver Range Rover Sport, fitted with winter tyres, waited for her. Forgetting to dampen her delight and excitement, Alexis rushed out of the hotel foyer like a young girl who'd just been told she could have a pony. The magnificent car, which was built for such conditions, soon navigated the Austrian and Swiss roads. By late afternoon they arrived at Chateau-d'Oex in Switzerland. After parking the car, he ran round to the passenger side to assist her as she vacated the high vehicle with the ice-covered stepping plates.

Continuing to support her by grabbing her arm, he led her forward. Within a short distance she could make out the collection of balloons for the nocturnal display. He approached one, its envelope now inflating rapidly, courtesy of the jets of hot air coming from the four gas burners. The propane tanks, finished in highly polished stainless steel, ticked slightly as they discharged their contents, feeding the voraciously hungry combustion chambers. As he came closer, two men jumped out of the basket and came forwards.

"Oh, pleased to see you again, Sir. She's nearly ready, and we stocked the provisions you asked for." Shaking their hands, he thanked the two men, then motioned to Alexis to follow him. Helping her into the basket, he then got in beside her.

"Don't tell me. Is this yours?" she said with unmasked wonder. "No, of course not, I just borrow it from a friend on special occasions. This is one of the highlights of the Aerostiers' calendar." The two assistants caught the conversation and looked at each other as the words appeared.

"The *what* calendar?"

"Oh, I think it's a French word for men messing about in hot air balloons."

"Yes, I guess so. Still, at least it beats the garden shed any day of the week. So, are we actually going up in this thing?" she asked nervously.

"I am hoping so, at least that's the general idea." He caught the frisson of fear that raced over the pretty face. "Look, if your number was up, we would have both gone off that cliff edge."

"Yes, thank you for that confidence-boosting speech, just what I wanted to hear. I take it you've done this before?"

"Well, I read the first two chapters of the manual and it got a bit boring, so I didn't bother with any more."

"Were those last chapters to do with landing, at all?"

"Whoops, yes, now you come to mention it, I knew I'd forgotten something."

Sensing that he was having just a bit too much fun with his teasing, she looked directly at him and suggested, "Come on then, what are you waiting for? Strut your stuff. Let's go."

She'd deliberately tried to pitch her voice at its most confident, though she was pleased that he could not see her gently trembling legs through the padded salopettes. Smiling confidently, he reached up to fire the burners more vigorously, and the whole assembly was now pulling restlessly against its tethering rope. A short time later he motioned to his two assistants that it was time to ascend and with a simple wave back, they released the fetters.

The balloon floated effortlessly upwards, a little slowly and sedately at first, but then it accelerated with an elating rush that rippled through her stomach. Spellbound, she looked round and saw the magnificent sight of at least twenty other balloons about to join them. The intense white, yellow and red flames given off by the combustion process produced copious quantities of heat, especially impactful in the gathering darkness. Four large jets of flame consumed the propane greedily, giving off a visceral roar as they did so. The envelope became pregnant with the hot air so formed and wanted to rise, to gain ascendancy over the ground, the snow and the sky. She saw the other balloons' burners doing the same. The illumination they created highlighting the folds of their fabric with a magical glow against the snow-saturated backdrop. As they rose, the burners were silenced. Ghostly yet silent apparitions ascended the heavens, in that moment freed from the Earth that had tried to constrain them. The sight was akin to a magical levitating spell that had been cast by a wizard with unseen, yet limitless power.

Looking up at the envelope, she read the logo.
"Event Horizon, is that the name of the balloon or the company or what? What does it mean? Is it the name of a company, your company? Your friend's company?"

He smiled patiently, as he could see by the light from the combustion that many questions queued within.

"Event horizon, so they tell me, is the edge of a black hole. This is where the escape velocity is equal to the speed of light, so that not even light can escape a black hole," he began, sensing that many more questions remained.

"Wow, clever stuff. So, did you think of this?"

"They say it's also the edge of reality, from the real to the unreal, where the laws of physics no longer apply."

Scrutinising him more carefully, he seemed to know just a bit too much about the things she witnessed first-hand. "Are you sure this isn't your balloon?"

Unable to wait for his answer, she raced round the basket from side to side. Each view appeared more exciting, more enchanting and more magical than the one that preceded it. She felt like a schoolgirl visiting a petting zoo with furry animals on all sides of the rectangular pen.

"Can I tempt you? Come on, how about some champagne and some truffles, or some food maybe? I got the lads to pack a picnic for us."

They ate and they drank. The bubbles from the champagne typically having an intoxicating effect, and her head soon became a little dizzy. Fascination accompanied by limitless curiosity still occupied her face. She'd been told, been warned, that he was a ladies' man, but this was taking things to a whole new level.

They travelled on through the valley for some time. She could see the beautiful, multi-coloured balloons glowing every time their burners were fired, so as to deny the hungry Earth its prey for some time longer. Her mobile phone clicking repeatedly as she took picture after picture, each successive image seemingly more wonderful than the last. It had been a long time since she'd spent a day like this, or, in effect, any day, like this.

All too soon, it was time to descend and his landing was unsurprisingly a model of accuracy and control. The Range Rover approached a few minutes after they'd landed and the two assistants came to help them and secure the basket, which still bobbed about restlessly as the balloon tried to respond to some of the gentle winds.

"Have you had a good flight, Sir?"

"Yes, marvellous thank you, Will. And thanks to you both for helping me."

Alexis became somewhat giddy from the champagne. Also, the heady mix of all pervading crisp clean mountain air, the snowy backdrop and, without doubt, excitement added its influence to her mood. "Are you sure this is not your balloon?"

"As I said, Alexis, I am very fortunate to have some wonderful friends, who are kind to me."

A short time later he was driving her back to her hotel. She sank back in the comfortable sumptuous leather seat and felt more relaxed and also, she considered later, more happy, than at any time since her mum had died.

As he came to a halt in front of her hotel he said, "Alexis, I'm leaving tomorrow. I have some business to attend to and will be travelling south to Dubrovnik. Can I tempt you to spend a few days with me? Come. You'll be welcome and the Adriatic is still warm even at this time of year."

"No, no thanks. I think I should be getting back home."

"I'm sure they could manage without you for another day or two?"

"Mm, not sure about that."

"Have you not got anyone whom you can rely on? Surely there are people you can trust?"

"Oh yes, of course. It's just my life, I guess."

"Very well then, it's settled. I'll collect you from your hotel tomorrow and we fly south."

"What's 'settled', I don't recall anything being 'settled'?"

"Don't you think, sometimes one has to be more spontaneous?"

"I'm not sure about that, either. I don't really 'do' spontaneous."

"Can you trust me, perhaps, and just go with it?"

"Now, that, I'm definitely not sure of, but I do want you to know I've had an amazing time and I cannot thank you enough for what's been a whirlwind 48 hours."

This was it. She'd find herself returning to those simple words, again and again in the coming days. He'd also hinted at the nature of her intractable bonds restraining a life that she could never foresee parting.

"You trusted me not to let you go off that cliff edge, and you trusted me in the balloon, and it's only the second time I've been up."

"That I definitely don't believe, about the balloon I mean."

He smiled at the fact that at least it was just the bit about the balloon that she was wary of.

"Okay then, it's settled, told you! If it's only my experience with the balloon, you are unsure of, then, surely, that must mean you agree that you can trust me! Absolutely, no more needs to be said?"

She now smiled at his persuasive and persistent logic.

"May I ask, why?"

"Why, what?"

"Why me?"

"*Why not you* I suppose is the answer."

A silence opened.

"I detect something of an air of mystery about you. Something of the night, perhaps."

"Wow, now I am really scared, too. Well then, surely, this is a good opportunity for you to find out more?"

"What if I don't like what I see, or what I find out?"

"Do you honestly think that's likely? I'm hardly going to pull someone off that mountain and then start treating her badly?"

"Perhaps that was your day off! Besides, for all I know you might be doing that on a regular basis. Pulling someone off a mountain, I mean."

He laughed. "Well, in that case, in a few days I'll have another day off. So, why not pop home to make sure everything is okay, feed your cat and water your plants. Then, tell you what, day after tomorrow, I'll send someone to collect you just outside the walls of Dubrovnik old town. If you are not there, then I'll know that you couldn't tear yourself away or you weren't that curious after all. And since you asked, I'm not sure I could do it again – catch someone going that fast off the edge of the mountain."

"I bet that's your party piece, saving out of control skiers! Very well, then, I may just be spontaneous, and fly in to Croatia, but if I am not there, then please don't wait."

"I can ask no more."

When she opened the door, the interior lights came on and she unfastened her seatbelt. Being consumed with insatiable curiosity about one further thing, she knew that she just had to satisfy it and the solution was close at hand. She leaned over and kissed him, before quickly vacating the car without turning back, so that he could not see the smile that now covered her face. Entering her hotel, she managed to catch a reflection of the large 4x4 in one of the mirrors in the foyer and saw that he paused for several long minutes, before driving off. Moreover, she couldn't help but wonder if, as the interior lights faded, he touched the cheek that she'd kissed.

Chapter VIII

Moment In Paradise

Catching the first flight to London the following morning, her head was in a whirl. So many thoughts, all conflicting, vied for her urgent attention, and she could make no sense of any of them. She immediately phoned Mr Forsythe. "I haven't got very far, I'm afraid. He certainly is the charmer all right, but I don't receive the impression we are dealing with a crook or a bad man."

"Maybe not, Miss, but do remember the people he associates with are the ones we are after and he is a good way to get access to them. I have a feeling that they are never far away. I hope I didn't say he was a bad man. It's the people around him we want. He is the key to the puzzle. Could we ask you please to tough it out for a few more days? I know it's a bit of an imposition, but you have got further than anyone else."

"Oh well, I suppose I could bear it for just a little while longer," she offered, being grateful that he wasn't able to see her broad smile, one that had been appearing with more frequency of late.

Alexis also met up with Maisie and Peter, her Head of Production.

The two employees looked at each other uncertainly. There was definitely something in the wind. They'd both known her for some years, having worked with her so closely that they could not miss the change in her. She'd always been bright, pleasant, hardworking and gave one hundred per cent, everything she had, to the business. However, they both recognised immediately that something new was afoot and it was by no means a subtle nuance, but something more significant. The obvious guess, that they made independently, was that during her travels she'd met someone and this person was wholly responsible for the unmistakable changes they witnessed. Both Maisie and Peter tried not to stare but somehow neither of them could help it, given the captivating new emotions exhibited by their boss and the pure fascination she'd in turn engendered in them. Whatever or whoever it was, they concluded, it could only be seen as a good thing. Each time she looked away they gave each other long looks and tapped each other knowingly as refreshing new facets of her mood and character presented themselves.

Somewhat reluctantly, a first in itself, they knew they had things to report about the business. Peter began, "My goodness, orders have really taken off. Looks like it was an inspired move to buy up that stock overhang of antique glass. The new sapphire blue range has been extremely popular; it's flying out of our warehouse, and especially in Switzerland, since you opened the new facility in Vevey."

"The other thing I have to tell you," Maisie confirmed, "our website is experiencing record numbers of hits. Interest from Canada and the States, the whole of North America is unparalleled and orders are coming in as soon as we can ship them. In fact, we may need to recruit some more personnel, in addition to the ones we have just taken on."

"Very well, perhaps we can make a decision on that in the near future? I need to be away again just for a few days," Alexis offered apologetically.

"Look, Alexis you never take holidays," started Maisie, but Peter also nodded in agreement, as they glanced quickly at each other, once again being aware of the thoughts they shared.

"Oh, I am so sorry to let you down."

"No, not quite what I meant," Maisie laughed. It was typical of her boss to assume she could not be spared. "Any news on the purchaser of our shares, Alexis?"

"No, Maisie, afraid not. Actually that's what I am working on, and why I need to be away," she said with more seriousness than she could summon inwardly.

"Just go, we will be fine here and we promise to look after it all while you're away, for however long that may be. We can always phone or Skype you, if we need your input," clarified Maisie.

The two employees sent each other knowing looks as they detected an enthusiasm on her face that they both recognised was, for the first time, in no way related to work. They eventually persuaded Alexis to leave work early, so that she could prepare for her departure the next day. Both of them stopped short of being too inquisitive, though questions ran within them like a burst water main. Maisie was unable to get Alexis on her own for long enough to ask some of the questions that now bubbled within. Unsatiated curiosity never sat easily on her consciousness, but ultimately she accepted that she'd just have to wait until the opportunity presented itself, whereupon she could quench it.

Arriving home to her empty house, Alexis prepared some food, but then discovered that she was not actually hungry. Sitting there manipulating her dinner with a fork, her thoughts were far removed. She recalled the beautiful mountains and wondered about the sun-drenched Adriatic. She finished packing quickly, it being a simple matter of removing winter clothes from her suitcase and replacing them with summer ones. She delayed going to bed for as long as she was able by reading, listening to music and even doing her usual trick of looking through the *Companies' Directory* hoping that it would calm her thoughts. Finally, she capitulated, telling herself that she was surely exhausted and that entering a deep and restful sleep would be a formality.

As events turned out, another night of restless turmoil awaited her. In some ways having a big bed and occupying it alone always made things worse, for one had too much space to move around in. Continuing to move and turn in the large bed some hours after closing her eyes, her brain had refused to take the hint. A steady torrent of questions flowed like water running over a dam. Inquisitiveness fed relentless and recurring streams of thoughts and queries that effectively precluded sleep.

Inevitably she returned constantly to the man she'd been sent to meet and to glean more knowledge of. He seemed so friendly, so plausible and so *damned nice*. And as for being unsafe in taxis, she concluded she'd be pleased to be alone with him in a taxi any time!

Here was the greatest uncertainty, for she'd caught the glances at her legs and her chest when she'd been in the chalet with him wearing one of his oversized T-shirts, which was discrete but not entirely unrevealing in its dimensions. Yet for all this he'd not made a move. She'd heard him pause outside her door, but had received the impression that he was simply making sure his guest was settled rather than about to make a frantic pass at her. Chance would be a fine thing. Also unsettling her were the sly looks between her Finance Director and Peter, her Head of Production. Was it that obvious she was behaving like a lovesick schoolgirl? Heaven knew she had a company to run and there was no time for speculative adventures with a man she hardly knew, even if he had risked his own life in order to stop her going off a cliff!

After many restless hours, ones where she rotated round her bed like a spinning top on a table, some semblance of order came to her. However, something much deeper stirred within and, though she would not remember it come the morning light, a fleeting smile came to her as she finally fell asleep.

A drizzly morning and the cold chill added to the misery induced in all those who looked up at the leaden skies. She was glad to be leaving for Dubrovnik, where the paper assured her, it was warm and sunny. It was especially uplifting for her to close the suitcase, which contained nothing but summer clothes. Any other thoughts were rapidly suppressed and it helped to remind herself of the unsavoury Mr Ciesciu. Leaving the house, she gave a slight shiver as the cold air swept round her bare legs, while distaste for this man coursed within. She just couldn't understand how Toby fitted in with such a person. Perhaps there was no way forward other than to simply ask him. Surely until she did, logic would dictate the utmost caution.

After catching a taxi, she boarded the first BA flight out of Gatwick to Croatia and landed there some two and a half hours later. Despite it being the end of February, warm sunshine greeted her as she disembarked at Dubrovnik airport. The very same sun had been bathing the whole of the Dalmatian coast for some weeks now. Following her instructions, she asked the taxi driver to drop her at the entrance to the medieval, walled city. Stopping just outside the impactful tall gates, he gently deposited her bags on the pavement, gratefully receiving his fare and a gratuity. Waiting there in warmth, she could picture the traders and travellers of hundreds of years gone by, who might have stopped at this very spot as they waited to enter the city. Whilst she continued to take delight in imagining the eclectic scene that must have existed in years gone by, a limping old man came up to her. His jovial face, showing signs of the twin damaging effects of sun exposure and age.

Even more weather-beaten was his small electric truck. With justifiable apprehension she looked down at the pristine white skirt that she'd chosen that morning. Perhaps it hadn't been a good idea to select summer clothes, after all. He placed her bags on the flat deck at the back, the whole thing resembling a milk float. The elderly chap motioned to her to get in, which she did with a graceful smile. He entered the driver's side while she wondered if her skirt would ever be the same again. The vehicle accelerated quickly and quietly under the urges of the electric motor, only a slight whirr betraying its labours. Within a few minutes he'd sped through the old town and approached the compact harbour.

Once again, her bags were deposited, but this time on the quayside. As she waited she looked down with some relief at the skirt, which seemed to have survived largely intact. The port was fairly quiet at this time of year. The numerous tenders from the massive cruise liners that would tie up along the wooden jetties were not expected until Easter.

Her full instructions followed, Alexis remained with steadily mounting excitement. Wondering what would happen next, she looked from face to face at the people enjoying the beauty of the 'pearl of the Adriatic'.

It was then that she saw him. She told herself that her breathlessness and racing pulse were purely down to relief at being in the right place after her journey. Toby's walk a little wide based, looking as though he'd just stepped out of his skis; later he explained that she'd witnessed his sea legs in action.

Coming along the quayside, he waved excitedly. She did her best to calm such thoughts and appear demure. He appeared even taller than she'd remembered. She reflected on those long legs that had enwrapped her own in order to save her. Looking down at the dark shorts and the striped T-shirt he wore, she noticed his complexion was already sun kissed in the short interval that he'd been here. As she stood there blinking expectantly in the late morning sunshine, she contemplated that safe in taxis or not, he was certainly not unattractive.

Standing in front of her, almost to attention, he gave an informal salute.

"I just love your wonderful hat," she offered, as she laughed at the admiral's cap he was wearing.

Touching the peak, she gently pulled it down a little more. He laughed, too, in unison while he touched the peaked cap and the gold embroidered ship's anchor emblazoned on the front.

"Oh, I don't claim to be an admiral or anything like that, but it does keep the sun out of my eyes. So you decided to risk it, then? Spontaneity won through?"

"I had nothing else to do, so I thought why not? How did you know whether to send your milk-float man or not?"

"Oh, I have a contact at Gatwick and he reported your name appearing on the flight manifest."

"Wow, being watched now, am I?"

He smiled. "Yes, Alexis, I'll have trouble tearing my eyes away from you."

Suddenly, blood rushed to her face to form the rapidly appearing blush. She was grateful for the sun, which she quickly looked toward in order to mask it.

A gleaming seascape stretched away from them, beyond the old town, far beyond the stone breakwater and into the distance. One or two small islands could be seen punctuating the glorious vista, like jewels embedded in blue enamel as it reflected the azure sky.

"So glad you could come."

"Oh, as I said, I thought, why not. It's also raining at home and very dull."

"I am so pleased you managed to tear yourself away from your work. Is that a hard thing to do?"

"Well, in truth I had Maisie, my FD and Peter, Head of Production, practically packing my bags for me. They told me I was due a holiday."

"So, then, we can't all be wrong."

"Not sure about that," she said, a little defensively as if she'd not quite thought through her own motives in living only for her work.
Changing the subject quickly, he suggested, "Well, I am sure a day or two will do no harm and I'll do my best to show you my favourite sights."

"So, where are we off to then?"

"Good question, come with me. How are your sea legs?"

"Sea legs, are we going on a boat?"

He grabbed her hand and led her along the wooden deck boards along the quayside. He stopped next to a gleaming white speedboat, dazzling as it reflected the sun's rays.

"Don't tell me you borrowed this from a friend, too?"

"Just how did you guess?"

"My, what friends you have. I must ask you more about those sometime. It seems everyone needs friends like yours."

"Perhaps they do," came his defensive reply.

"I must warn you, I am a terrible sailor," she admitted, nervously.

"Oh, don't worry. The Adriatic is really calm. You'll be fine when we get there."

"Where are we going?"

"A voyage of discovery."

"Okay then, admiral, let's go."

The speedboat was in pristine condition without a spec of dirt. Its sharp bow pointed out to sea with purpose and a hint of exciting moments to be discovered. She noted the polished teak deck, complete with shining chrome fittings. Holding her hand with his strong grip, one that had already proved itself within the last few days, he helped her climb into the front seat, which was shaped like an armchair, in soft white Italian leather. A few moments later he returned with her bags, which he stowed. After untying the plaited cord, he nudged the boat away from the quayside, jumped on board then pulled up two of the marine fenders, also on white cords. He sank into the captain's seat.

He looked at her and smiled. "Are you ready?"

Nodding pleasantly, she did her best not to look either frightened or uncertain, although she'd never been on a speedboat before and certainly nothing like this. Twin Yamaha engines fired in concert, their grumble felt as much as heard. As the fuel came in with a rush, the slight irregular note was replaced by a growl. Opening the throttles a little more brought movement. The pumps spat out water from the boat in disgust at the medium it wanted to reign over. The couple made smooth but sedate progress out of the time-hallowed harbour. The engines were now making a smoother rhythmic 'phut', 'phutting' noise as they made ready for a demonstration of their unremitting power.

As soon as they were clear of the harbour walls, he removed his cap and found, from the locker, two baseball caps and two pairs of sunglasses. Passing one of each to her, he put the others on. As soon as the throttles were opened further, the growl became a roar. The prow of the boat then lifted, for it became as an arrow, built for cutting through water at prodigious speed. The engines bit by the stern so that the whole boat rocketed along causing a vast quantity of spray to their side. Emphatically, the smooth sea parted compliantly, forming no barrier to the sleek craft. Its advance readily measured by the water, which foamed and crested in their wake with nearly as much excitement as shown by his passenger. Some bobbing occurred, the vessel almost leapt from the water while it progressed, adding a tantalising blend of uncertainty and exhilaration to their trip.

The gentle spring day refused to be outdone by the craft coursing through the waves. It bathed them in a brilliant and warm light as they shot forwards: the illumination and the spray creating cascades of rainbows to accompany them as they did so.

He looked at her, the sun-drenched hair now flailing wildly behind her, despite the cap. She leant back in her chair while she relaxed. Her face was poised to gather more of the life-giving heat; a broad smile with the even white teeth very much in evidence. She caught his look, part fascination, part curiosity and was obviously keen to impress. She couldn't think for the moment why, but knew that such thoughts would return later.

"Not too fast?" he asked as he turned to her, and the speedboat surged onward like a charger galloping over the seas.

Laughing by way of reply, as her head came back, she shook her head gently from side to side so that the roaring wind and slipstream could tousle her glorious hair. After a few minutes they approached the small islands that had been visible from the shore. He continued to charge westward, soon leaving them in their wake as the mighty engines refused to yield.

Alexis would reflect on this moment in the days ahead, when her life lay in ruins, that this had been the happiest she'd been in a very long time. Indeed, she considered, if paradise could be distilled into one single minute of one's life, then, without hesitation, this would be the one she would choose.

For the time being, however, the sun glinted dazzlingly, being reflected by the wrap-around sunglasses while the young woman looked up at the infinity of the blue sky and at the handsome man, doing his best, but failing in the attempt, not to try to impress her. Now her hair was somewhat awry, but lit gloriously nevertheless by the bright vista that seemed to resonate within, as had the majestic mountain and the ethereal night she'd witnessed from the balloon just a couple of days ago.

Just when she thought that the day, and this man, could yield no more surprises, she saw the super yacht. Though it was just down from the horizon, she guessed that this was their destination. The engines seemed to climax in an ecstasy of pulsating noise as he corrected their course for a rendezvous.

Even at this distance, the beautiful craft looked huge. She could make out its gleaming white superstructure, the radar pods and navigation equipment and the sleek, swept hull of navy blue. Alexis shook her head incredulously. The nearer they got to the striking vessel, the more impressed she became. She estimated that the yacht was not far off 100m in length. Toby throttled the engines back. The speedboat grumbled while it slowed to a crawl, its bow dipped as it sulked at making more contact with the clear sea shimmering placidly around them. Approaching from the rear, she saw the aft stowage area, a floating harbour, which was large enough to accommodate not only the speedboat but also two jet skis and the launch that it already contained.

Toby stood to gain a better view and then carefully swung the boat round so as to approach in the lee of the yacht, which remained at anchor. Within a few minutes, he tied up the boat on the aft deck. Using the white plaited rope, he quickly swept the knots round the mooring cleats. These beautiful pieces of hardware, which were of brightly polished stainless steel, remained hot to the touch as they failed to completely reflect the intense sunshine. The glare was so strong that it hurt one's eyes to look at them.

Having made the boat secure, he then returned in order to assist her. She stood somewhat precariously on the seat and after stabilising his own weight; he used both his arms to guide her onto the aft deck.

Making the final step with a little jump, she stood next to him. "Don't tell me, this is just a friend's too?"

"How did you guess?"

"Mm, I'm not sure about that, either," she offered, with her intense blue eyes now reflecting the bright seascape.

"Tell me, do you believe anything I tell you?"

She laughed. "Not sure that I do!"

He feigned a hurt look over the handsome face.

"Well, I'm here, aren't I?" she offered by way of apology.

"I can see we'll just have to do our best to change your mind."

"I won't hold my breath," she advised with the playful grin that visited her face between intense smiles.

He showed her up the stairs and onto the rear lower deck. While they had been talking, four of the ship's crew had turned out on the rear deck to greet them. Two young men and two women, each wearing blue baseball caps, white shirts and navy shorts. He introduced her as they passed them one by one. They then went about loading Alexis' bags and making secure the speedboat in preparation for their departure.

"How many crew does your 'friend's' boat have?"

"Ten in total, so he tells me, and you'll meet some of the others in a minute. I'll give you the grand tour. In fact we'll find

Captain Richards first and hopefully we'll set course. He'll be fettling his engines or seeing to his bilge pumps, or something similar."

He introduced her to the captain and some additional crew.

"We'll be getting underway in just a minute, if that meets with your approval, Sir?" the captain suggested.

"Any time at your convenience, Bill."

Toby escorted her to her cabin, which was known as a Guest Stateroom. This was a magnificent suite, complete with large bed, long rectangular window and a luxury en-suite bathroom.

"My goodness! This is a real home from home, not quite what I was expecting. The amount of space alone, one could swing round a big cat in here."

"Oh, we don't like to rough it, you know, and since we did away with the hammocks strung over the cannons, there's been a lot more room."

"*Rough it* were the last words I was thinking. This is palatial."

"If you are pleased, then I am too. I hope you'll be very comfortable. You can go anywhere apart from the forward saloon, where we plot world domination."

For a second she missed the joke, and then laughed. "Yes, I saw the name of the boat on the back *Ma Puissance*. What's that? My strength? My power? Something like that?"

"Oh you know, rich folk, they like these grand names. Coming back to the boat, of course, means you can go anywhere. The engineer doesn't really like anyone going into his engine room, but then again he doesn't really like anyone, anyway, though I am sure you'll manage to charm him, somehow."

"And why do you think that?"

"Oh, just a wild guess," he offered, as he tried to suppress his smile.

"Where are me and the engineer headed then?"

Now he did smile. "We'll be there shortly, perhaps I should say, you'll be there shortly."

"I just hope this chap is devilishly handsome, and a good skier, of course."

"As are all our staff, and especially good at…"

"Stop it, *right* there, don't remind me," she shuddered as she recalled her descent of the precipitous black run.

"Sorry, couldn't resist it."

Just at that point she felt the engines start with momentary vibration coursing through the massive craft. This soon gave way to a hum, which continued as the boat's anchors were weighed and the super yacht almost shuddered with its exertions. Further complex sounds came to her for a few more seconds as the rudders responded to the new course and without further ado they were underway. Alexis felt the vessel turn and through the large tinted windows she could see the sunshine now appearing off their starboard quarter while they journeyed south. As they did so, the sun began its descent through the clear afternoon sky.

"Come on, then, let's go back on deck!" Their guest raced like an excited schoolgirl on a trip to an ice cream parlour. The sight was majestic as the sun deepened in colour. Its awesome power was now filtered more obliquely through the atmosphere, appearing to exchange brightness for size while it slowly sank ever nearer the horizon. He showed her the way to the sundeck, which was the highest deck on the super yacht. From here she could get an even better view of the beautiful coastline.

Alexis glanced up at the intense blue sky, surely a miracle in itself, if one could just pause to appreciate it. She noticed the two whip aerials that sloped backwards from the rear, seemingly extending all the way to the heavens, together with the spinning radar boom that appeared to sweep the almost imperceptible curve of the horizon. Aft of the boat she noted some of the white foaming of the waves as the propellers conveyed them at a more sedate, but no less exhilarating pace than the speedboat.

Chapter IX

Calypso

Just before sunset, they made Cavtat harbour and she could feel the grumbling as the anchors were dropped.

"*Ma Puissance* is a little too large for the harbour. So, the captain will anchor here. Where would you like to dine? In or out, or perhaps I should say on-board or on land?" Toby asked.

"No doubt your friend has a Michelin starred chef chained to a stainless steel bench below decks," she wondered.

"Actually, it's the engineer with a big microwave."

"Now, there's a tempting offer. But would you mind if we go ashore? I am certain that your friend knows a nice bijou fish and chip shop, where we can get some mushy peas and a meat pie?"

"Mm perhaps you'd better stay here with the engineer after all."

"What, and stop you from showing off? That'll never do. Come on then, impress the girl!"
Her smile rose like the first morning of Creation as she moved her upturned palms away from her sides, shrugging her shoulders while she signified her eagerness to learn more. "Let's go ashore?"

"Very well then, I'll meet you on the aft deck at 7:30."

"Shouldn't you say eight bells or something like that?"

"No, actually, I'm sure it should be seven."

"Oh no! This is your boat isn't it? How else would you know about bells and things like that?"

"Look, the number of people I bring here, I have to impress them, somehow."

"Now then, *that* I do believe."

"Ha, at last! Something the girl believes," as he continued. "Right, I'll get my party frock on and see you back here?"

"Very well then," she offered, "How you dress when you are on holiday is your business. I just hope you've got the legs for it. Actually, those legs are not bad." She looked down at his shorts. "I can see I'll have competition."

"No, I think not, Alexis. Let's just say the prettiest girl in Cavtat has just arrived!"

"Wow, I am speechless, thank you. I suspected you'd be a bit of a charmer."

"What else, I'm a man aren't I?"

"I'll just go and get a quick shower, perhaps make yours extra cold?" she suggested, as he laughed.

An hour later, she stepped up from her guest suite, the spiky shoes making an uneasy noise on the decking. She found him waiting for her, sipping a gin and tonic. Standing next to him while the last remnant of sunshine dipped below the horizon, she was mesmerised at its final serenade to the day. He offered her a drink, then, as his eyes took in more of her appearance, he moved back a couple of feet so that he could gaze at her more easily.

He smiled. "Well, businesswoman scrubs up nicely."

"Not bad? And hopefully without too much scrubbing."

"Wow Alexis, you look wonderful."

"Not bad for someone who'd nearly been off a cliff?" she wondered.

"Don't start that again, but yes, quite right! Not bad at all."

"Well, thanks for the compliment. That's one or two within the last hour. You aren't going to get giddy on me are you?" she asked a little flirtatiously.

She smiled back in his direction, thoughts of a similar nature being kept tightly under wraps as she looked at him. The beautifully cut jacket seemed perfectly at home on his muscular frame. Realising that further words would reveal more than was wise, she relied on her disarming smile to provide a safer response than anything else.

Two of the crew had retrieved the launch, which was a larger but more sedate form of travel than the speedboat, from the floating harbour. It was tied up and waiting for them by the stern. They departed under the ambient light, which was still perfectly satisfactory, despite the fact that the sun had disappeared below the horizon some minutes before. Having set off, they made slow but steady progress towards the land.

She marvelled at the picturesque but small harbour, and the village of Cavtat, which was grateful for the short break from the hordes of tourists who would appear a little later in the year.

They went ashore and both the boat and the spiky heels were thankful when she stepped out on to the stone breakwater of the quayside.

"I think I'd better carry these on our return journey," as she pointed to the shoes.

He cheekily replied that the boat had only sprung a leak in the form of a couple of tiny holes, and it would take at least an hour or two before it sank.

They walked towards the restaurant he had recommended. Evergreen poplars lined the harbour frontage and from there they crossed over the quiet road to approach the bistro. Rusty lanterns gave off a yellow light bathing the quayside in a charming glow as others reflected off the calm sea. She saw the super yacht dipping very gently in the evening swell, some distance away.
"Don't worry, the engineer will wait up for you," he offered, catching her direction of gaze.

"He'd better, I'm hoping to help him polish those engines when I get back."

Suddenly she changed the mood. "May I ask you? Why me? Why all this," she spread her arms widely as they walked. "Why now, why here, why – everything!"

"Alexis that is a lot of 'whys'. 'Why not?' I suppose is the answer. Amazing, intelligent, pretty girl, fantastic skier; good with engines and microwaves; generous friends, wonderful food and glorious weather: does it have to be more than that? Surely, it must beat work any day of the week?"

"But, of course. Though I live for my work, I do realise that there is more to life than my job. My business is what has made me, what drives and sustains me and I do accept that I'd be lost without it; this, for sure, is why I must protect it from those who would like to take it from me. After my mum died, I had nothing. Starting my company saved me when I had no one to turn to. That business became my companion as well as my saviour."

She glanced at him in that moment. Detecting that her words had saddened him more than politeness would have sanctioned, but nevertheless, she was convinced in that second he was about to reach out for her in order to hug her. Something checked him in that scintilla of time and instead the deep blue eyes became even larger and deeper as he stared at her.

Knowing that few words would serve at that point, he managed, "I am so sorry, Alexis," as soon as he could be certain that his voice would not waver.

She took a deep breath to steady her tumultuous thoughts, then continued. "However, be that as it may, I think that we both know that there is more here than meets the eye?"

"We do?"

Suddenly, he reached towards her, lightly touching her arm to emphasise the point he was trying to make. She gave a little jump as the light touch went through her like a palpable current, doing her best to disguise it.

"Can we make a deal?"

"Go on?"

"We spend the next day or two, however many you would like to stay, talking about everything and anything apart from the words you were just about to say?"

"But those words, we both know, I suspect, are why I am here. Am I here for any other reason?"

He smiled. His aquamarine eyes met hers seemingly for the very first time, as he looked at her in that instant. The gaze so intense yet so open, that words would have failed at this point had he not blinked when the waiter appeared in order to show them to their table. Otherwise, he reflected later, that that expression, staring at his very own Calypso, would have existed on his face until the seas had boiled dry.

"Please let's just spend these next few days, friend to friend, world-travelling, lonely adventurer to hard-working, pretty girl."

"I can't believe you are lonely?"

"Deal?"

"Very well, with one condition."

"Name it."

"We meet in London at a time and place of my choosing and I can then ask you all the things that I was about to."
She thought in that second, as the words escaped her lips, that she'd overworked the deal, one that surely he was not about to agree to.

Yet, her worries were unfounded, because his smile came forth, after an imperceptible delay, and he nodded in the time it took her racing heart to form a couple of beats. "Yes, agreed."

"Agreed?"

"Yes, do you want me to sign a contract or perhaps swear on the Hot Air Balloon Handler's Manual, something along those lines?"

"I just happen to have one here." Then she laughed, and continued, "No, your word will be just fine with me."

"So, tell me, are you lonely?" she just had to return to the tantalising piece of information that he'd let slip.

"No, not really, are you?"

"Well, I have my work."

"Your work! So, that's okay then, and what else?"

"What else is there?"

"Tell me in a few days?"

"I hope I'm not about to be swept off my feet. Am I?"

"No, I think that would take much more than I could offer."

She smiled disarmingly, once again, but instinctively knew that this was not the case.

As they sat at their table, the restaurant owner came forward in something of an excited rush, greeting Toby effusively like a long-lost brother. As soon as Toby introduced Alexis, similar treatment was reserved for her. He kissed her repeatedly, much to her embarrassment.

The owner left them to study the menu and Alexis decided to quiz Toby. "You are so well known here it's almost as if you are at your local. Are you sure that boat isn't yours? Look, you can tell me, I'm just as nice to multi-millionaires as I am to penniless ski dropouts, you know." Her smile danced with delight, on the pretty face, as she gazed at him.

"I am sure you are," he offered, sincerely. "Let's just say the owner lets me borrow his boat whenever I want."

"Everyone needs a friend like that!"

Courses appeared and were quietly whisked away as they talked. They talked while more lights blinked on across the bay and then started to fade. They continued to talk until well after the few remaining tourist boats had departed, until the harbour-front restaurant had emptied and still they talked.

A few minutes later, upon looking at his large black watch with white numerals and hands, he noticed that it was well after midnight. The waiter dutifully asked them for about the fifth time if they'd like more coffee and was almost unable to hide his relief when Toby said that he'd like the bill. The owner at this point reappeared, looking a little dishevelled as if he'd been snoozing in another room.

Leaving the restaurant, they walked from one end of the small, but beautiful harbour, to the other. Some time in the early hours of the new day, they found the launch. The air was still clear but chilly as the clear skies had remained overhead. Toby draped his jacket over her bare shoulders to keep her from shivering as he helped her to get back into the boat. She held the shoes in her hands, while he offered her reassurance that as it was still afloat, there was probably little cause for concern.

There followed some magical days where they cruised up the Dalmatian coast and during this time no mention was made of the subject about which they'd declared an amnesty. This was especially useful for her as it meant that one big source of anxiety was removed at a stroke. Given that he'd agreed to return to London, her mission was technically over. She could pass it back to Mr Forsythe and hopefully still gain insight as to why her company was in danger.

Curiosity continued to burn and she took every available opportunity to study him. He couldn't have been friendlier, more helpful, more delightful to talk to, nor more easy on her eyes. However, there remained something of mystery about him. She had to constantly remind herself of his associate who was still buying shares in her company. The price of which had long since risen to what Maisie would refer to as nosebleed levels. The other thing that she kept wondering about was the fact that she'd been warned about his interest in, and appetite for, members of the opposite sex. Conversely, she felt almost disappointed that she could detect stark trace of it. Indeed, for a while, she'd concluded that far from being unsafe in taxis as Mr Forsythe had quaintly put it – he would, without doubt, be safe to travel with in a taxi or in anything else for that matter. She decided one night just before sleep overcame her that he'd probably be safe in a harem.

Her initial assumption, which was the obvious one, was that he was probably gay. Not that this perturbed her in the least. Then she'd seen the way he looked, gazed into her eyes, noticed everything that she wore, and especially when legs or chest were on show. As curiosity grew, she couldn't resist getting a little closer, had whispered in his ear and had even hugged him each night before she found her cabin. Even after a week of being more or less continuously in each other's company, she was no nearer to answering this one burning question that tasked her almost as much as the ones about his business associates and activities.

Their accompaniment during the day was the bright sunshine, which slowly became stronger every day as it rose to new heights in the heavens each time it appeared. By night they met on deck and witnessed beautiful sunsets, and despite the variety of topics that they discussed at this time, each became quiet as they observed one of nature's enduring miracles.

A day or two later she asked that the boat be brought about so that she could begin her return to London. A couple of days later they approached the charming harbour at Cavtat and the captain brought his boat in as far as was wise.

All too soon it was time for her departure and the entire yacht's company turned out on the aft deck to see her off. The launch was loaded with her bags; she came forward with more nervousness and haste than they'd noted before. Alexis had become quite proficient at navigating narrow companionways and stairs. Even when the swell caused the yacht to pitch, roll or yaw unexpectedly, she never had a problem. That final day, however, it was perhaps her heel that had caused her to stumble at the very top of the aft stairway, just as the boat's crew waited for her. Within a split second, she was caught by a tall, handsome young man. His strong, muscular arms not only arrested her fall, but also set her back on the steps in less time than it took to blink. She thanked him somewhat breathlessly, as she recovered her poise.

Upon boarding the launch and sitting next to Toby, she asked him who the handsome man was. "Oh that's the engineer," he confirmed with a mischievous smile.

"Wow, missed out there! Can I cancel my trip home?"

"Yes, of course," he offered, laughing, hoping that her words held more substance than jest.

Docking in the harbour, he made ready to leap out on to the quayside to tie up the boat. Once secure, he helped her ashore and gave her bags to the taxi driver who waited to take her to the airport. Finally, as the cabbie started his engine, Toby stood next to her on the quayside.

"Thanks so much for the past few days and also my ski trip, not to mention my escape from a grisly death – twice, or so it would seem," she began brightly but a nuance of sadness had crept in to dampen her melodic voice.

"Alexis, it's all been a pleasure and you'll be welcome to return. I hope you've seen that though work is important it's okay to enjoy yourself, just once in a while?"

"Perhaps you're right. I'll have to think about that one. In any event, I have had a wonderful time and you obviously have some great friends."

"Indeed I do. So, as promised and arranged I'll see you in London next week."

He held out his hand, but she bypassed this, stretched up towards him, kissing him, before she spun round and walked towards the taxi. Desperately wanting to turn round and look back at the scene, she knew that had she done so, her eyes and her expression would have betrayed her. She waited instead until she was seated in the back of the taxi, behind a tinted window where she could look back at the beautiful harbour of Cavtat, the astounding yacht and the man who intrigued her much more now than when they'd first met.

Chapter X

Deception

Alexis returned to London Gatwick, telling herself that she was desperate to return to work and to see how the business was faring. When she left the terminal building in order to find her taxi, miserable weather awaited. Looking up at the dull grey skies of early March, she shivered as her bare legs encountered much lower temperatures than they'd experienced in the past few days. This and the steady drizzle served to trigger recent memories of much prettier vistas, which only induced unhappiness in their wake. It seemed in that moment as if she'd spent her life sheltering from the rain. Even worse, it always appeared to be a Monday.

'I'll feel better when I get back to work,' she decided, reasoning that getting back into her old routine would be the way forward. She went out for some food and returned to her house. Automatic tasks that didn't require a lot of concentration, like unpacking the shopping, allowed more restless thoughts to creep back in. She'd always liked living here and had never felt lonely – until now.

She saw the bright red tablet that Mr Forsythe had given her on the sofa and she knew that looking through it would remind her of the job she'd been sent to do. At least she'd accomplished her mission and Toby was due to fly in to London Airport. They would soon be discussing things with him on home turf without the distraction of gleaming seascapes and miles of pristine pistes that were calling out to be skied. The businesswoman told herself that there was absolutely no reason for her heart skipping along in this fashion other than the fact that she was about to glean knowledge that Mr Forsythe had assured her would further their mutual aims – she in protecting her company and he in gaining information about the elusive, thus far, bullet-proof oligarch.

Activating the tablet, she read through the articles that had been stored there and also the numerous links that had been conveniently organised in lists for her. It was at this point, however, that she noticed something strange. Though the links led to useful information, modern search engines would retrieve this data in much more detail and also more quickly. Of course they were simply arranged in this way to save her time. On further inspection, however, she noticed that many of the links had a familiar look and feel to them as if they had been created artificially, and by the same person.

Doubts fed suspicion and she quickly found her own laptop. Within seconds she was searching with one of the popular search engines. The material thus uncovered was available to anyone who had a mind to search on any of the keywords she'd encountered over the past few days, and contained much less information than the links that had been placed for her use on the tablet. She searched on the logo on the side of the hot air balloon and also the super yacht, *Ma Puissance*. Next to nothing was available on any of the public search engines, apart from the fact that a company called 'Horizon Enterprises' owned them both. Searching in turn on the name of this company also yielded little by way of results. She knew that any quoted company of any size was by law required to calculate, publish and file a set of company accounts, just as she did.

The only companies that were not required to do this were small ones owned by one person with one or two employees, or private businesses, which operated beyond the constraints of Stock Exchange and Companies House rules. Very wealthy private individuals, or even families, if they were of any size, would often own the latter type. Even this discovery did not induce undue suspicion until she searched for his name. Very little information came up and suspicion rose within. Of course it was within anyone's prerogative to keep a low profile and not to advertise one's presence or activities in the financial pages or on Twitter or Facebook feeds. She admired people like herself who led discrete and quiet lives away from the public's scrutiny. It was, however, the difference between the two types of articles: the ones that had been prepared for her on the tablet, and unrestrained searches, which were available to anyone on any search engine. It was almost as if she'd been presented with a trail of breadcrumbs – breadcrumbs put there purely for her to follow. She wondered why this was so and why she had been chosen – a person who surely was of no interest to anyone.

Realising that there was now one other vital piece of evidence that she just had to investigate, she grabbed the blacker-than-black credit card with the raised relief in seemingly pure molybdenum, and then her car keys. Driving down to her local bank, she knew they had a cash machine where within seconds she could discover much more about the unusual card. She waited for the current user to finish his transaction and approached the machine with a curiosity that was by now overwhelming. Using the PIN they'd given her, she withdrew £100 in cash and waited eagerly for the paper slip that the machine generated. The slip duly confirmed that she had withdrawn £100 but, in tiny print along the bottom, it informed her that she could withdraw a further £9,900 that day. Alexis surmised that she could probably withdraw another £10,000 each and every day, until she tired of such a thing.

Almost forgetting to collect her car, she had started walking back to her house. Then she remembered that she'd wanted the answers so quickly that she'd driven rather than walked down to the local bank. Conclusions now ran with her questions and created unrest, coupled with alarm. So, an elaborate and targeted scheme had been set up backed with massive funding. She'd never heard of nor seen such a credit card and although she mixed occasionally with very wealthy people, she doubted whether they had either.

Two questions ran through her and were unstoppable. 'Why me, and for what reason?'
These two questions continued to haunt her as she went to her sizeable but lonely bed. She hoped that by turning out all the lights in her large and quiet house, she'd be favoured with at least a little sleep. However, a steady stream of questions continued to queue within. These in turn fed a multitude of other thoughts that effectively precluded such a thing, until the small hours, whereupon she managed an hour of restless dreams.

Just before her tortured and fitful sleep began she was certain of only one thing. Toby would be arriving in London very soon and she was determined to seek even more answers from him than she'd planned. It appeared that Mr Forsythe also had a lot of explaining to do and she was now ready and waiting for the two of them. Giving a little shiver under her warm duvet, she realised that she could no longer tell what was real, if any of it, and what was a lie – probably all of it. One vast nexus of lies was the answer that would fit all of her questions.

*****

Half a dozen people sat round the large table in the offices at Salford Quays. The hour was late and they'd been working since 7am. Everyone was tired and the young woman at the head of the table was exhausted. She sighed and rubbed her forehead, hoping that by doing so she'd be able to summon a little more energy, more concentration or at least to wake up and discover that the whole thing had been a bad dream. The four interactive whiteboards that filled the far wall were full of diagrams, flow charts and many computations of probability. They'd been revised and re-worked time and time again. The details that they contained and the answers the calculations provided, cast nothing but worry on those who stared relentlessly at them, as if by scrutinising with more vigour would somehow alter the conclusions that they had all individually arrived at.

Sitting furthest from those screens, she was more acutely aware and more worried by them. The video camera blinked with a tiny green light as the large panel on the wall flared into life.

She dispensed with the usual niceties; there was some difficult ground to be covered. "Please look at the figures I am sending through to you now. Whichever way we take it, from this point onwards, it could go wrong and badly. We are out of our depth here, dangerously so. This is not what we do. Surely we intervene only if and when we have a high probability of success – not this." She pointed with distaste at the boards and screens. "I thought we had planned for different outcomes, of course, but this is all over the place. Are we not about to toss a match on a pool of petrol and hope that our house will be warmer without burning down?"

She looked at the largest screen, the one that summarised all the information that painstaking analysis had revealed to them. "Forgive me, I have to advise that we cut and run now, before someone gets hurt and badly; before you get hurt."

She saw his image nod in the display panel. He also looked tired and worried, as might someone who couldn't swim in finding that they'd strayed into deep water. He began, "I have had a word with Lord 'B'. I have conveyed your concerns to him; concerns which I share.
I've suggested that we bail out now. We do have at least partial success. He is not happy, however, and didn't want a partial solution. He says that we are supposed to be the best and we'd better start proving it."

"Have you told him that further work will put people at risk?"

He remained quiet and she continued, "Have you told him that you, in particular, will be put at highest risk, with a 95% probability, of physical and emotional injury?"

"Yes, I have."

"And?"

"He still wants us to commence phase three. He told me that he expects results, not excuses. He says that if we don't come through, then he'll expose us in the national newspapers"

She smiled for the first time. Although, this was not unusual when she spoke with him on any occasion, no matter how dark the day had become, or how tired she was, it, perhaps, signified more that the young woman was always at her very best when the situation was dire and apparently irretrievable.
"The cheeky bugger. It seems we have a gun held to our heads too, then! Very well, as he insists, you know that I'll do all that I can, but when it's over, when it's all over, I am *so* going to tell you 'I told you so'. You know that, don't you?"

"Don't you always say that when it goes wrong?"

"You are a cheeky bugger, too. Come on now, have I ever said that?" she scanned the room expectantly – the other five people all smiled, despite their exhaustion, but nodded their heads in support.

He smiled all too briefly, and then a far more serious expression overtook him as grim reality dawned.

"May I ask you," she looked sharply at him again, her piercing eyes now homing on him despite the video cameras, which rendered such things less distinct. "You know that this could turn quite nasty, for you especially. Are you prepared for that?"

There was a lengthy pause. She could see him holding his breath as he waited for her next words.

"Can I also ask?"

She hesitated, but the two people had known each other for long enough for each to know that she would continue.

"I have to ask… have you been compromised personally?"

Once again there was a gap in the conversation, the silence opening brutally as it existed between them.

"I'm sorry, but I need to know. And I need you to tell me, now."

It was the little glance away from the video camera that supplied her answer – more so than any words. She felt a waterfall of sadness cascade right through her, for she saw the truth, in that moment, whatever his words. Truth that she'd suspected some time before.

He shook his head a little too enthusiastically, as if movement would cover his tracks, and obscure his emotions.

"Of course not, I'm still on mission." She understood that pressing him more would only force him to admit what she already knew. To extract such a confession from him at this late hour would be both cruel and unproductive.

She continued, "Very well, then. If you are absolutely certain, then in that case, I'll accept your instructions."

They both knew this was important. It was a device that she'd used only once in the previous ten years. Formal instructions meant that she would not be held responsible if things went belly up. She would be exonerated in any enquiry that would conclude that she was simply acting on orders and she'd live to work and fight another day. She did not want to attract blame, even though she believed it was unlikely, in any event. Simply wanting to clear her conscience, she saw with some prescience that this was the only thing she'd have left in the days ahead.

"Yes, then please do," came from the speaker, "accept this as a formal instruction."

Doing her utmost, she tried to re-create the smile, to obscure the sadness that overwhelmed her, for she could see that in those thirty seconds she'd lost everything. "Very well, we'll put phase three in place and will start tonight."

The screen went blank. One or two people in the room looked crestfallen. Despite the late hour, there was still much work to do. Standing up, she clapped her hands. "Very well, then, you all heard the man. Phase three is 'go'. Begin at once."

She wasn't in any way religious, but if she had been, then, she accepted that she'd be on her knees in that moment deep in prayer. She could only hope much less perfect skills than Divine intervention would keep them all safe.

Without further discussion her team of five left the room, each being aware of their assigned role. One of their number drove straight to Manchester Airport and boarded a plane.

Remaining in the room, she gazed ahead of her not really focussing. Now no longer seeing the present, she stared straight into a vision of the future. She understood that three separate but restless ghosts were about to be awoken that would not only destroy herself but also the two main protagonists in this story. They'd all now entered a lethal cul-de-sac. Their client had insisted that they go forward when all their calculations and elegant planning warned of a disastrous outcome, for everyone involved.

Chapter XI

Sterling Effort

Early morning sunshine was even more intense in Kyrenia. Mr Ciesciu was hungry and he'd come ashore so that he could visit his favourite restaurant, just by the old castle, near Kyrenia port. Being sick and tired of on-board dining, he knew that he would fire his chef as soon as a replacement could be found. He was alone apart from four minders who accompanied him, each wearing ill-fitting suits that made them look more uncomfortable, but strangely more thuggish.

As a matter of course he was given his preferred table and he looked out at the port and the sun-drenched vista, which was not unusual for this part of Cyprus at this time of year. In fact, early March was his favourite time to visit. Few words were spoken, but the proprietor knew his place. At their first meeting, now some years ago, little explanation was provided to him apart from whether he was serious about keeping his business or not. From that day onwards he'd known exactly what was to be expected from him.

The restaurateur was frantically engaged in a whirlwind of activity. He'd scrubbed the table and made sure that pristine white linen covers were used throughout. He remembered the day when Mr Ciesciu had found a slight stain on his napkin and he'd stormed out in a rage, but only after overturning the whole table. Two of his minders had remained behind in order to make sure that the owner understood that this was his one and only chance to provide an 'acceptable' service and no further warnings would be given. They'd then assured the trembling man that next time, many more tables would be overturned.

That particular day, all the other diners were ignored whilst the owner and all his staff made sure that the table was as spotlessly clean and as well presented as a scrub nurse's instruments in an operating theatre. Under no circumstances would he be foolish enough to challenge the richest and most powerful man to grace the harbour, whatever demands were made of him. Far better to put up with the cruel and bad-mannered client; attempt to provide a service with a smile, than to risk his wrath.

Mercifully, the restaurant was quiet and he'd only had to move one couple from the table that Mr Ciesciu always sat at and a family of four from the table usually occupied by his minders. The proprietor raced round the restaurant instructing waiters and kitchen staff to the exacting requirements of their non-paying, but uninvited guest. He understood, too, that today's visit would without doubt prove expensive for him, and he could only hope that he had food of sufficient quantity and quality to give his 'special' guest, who also had an insatiable appetite, before one even considered his four minders. In a quieter moment, he reflected on the fate of his best waitress who had unfortunately attracted the attention of the Russian and who'd subsequently refused to return to her job.

Everything was going to plan and the important man was eating with his usual voracious style as someone might, who'd been lost on a desert island and had just found a crate of food that'd washed up. At that moment a medium-height young man walked into the restaurant. He looked a little too pale to be a resident and had obviously not been in Turkish Northern Cyprus for long. The owner surveyed him carefully, never having seen him before. Moreover, he looked as if he was probably from Europe, most likely England. Of most significance, however, was the fact that he was heading straight for the Russian who was still eating. Time stopped in that instant, for a mistake was about to be committed of epic and very damaging consequences for the stranger. It was too late to warn him. Unfortunately he would learn the folly of his actions very soon. Wearing a somewhat creased linen suit, he carried a slim aluminium case. The owner wondered how crumpled the suit would be when they'd finished with him. He could only hope that they would remove him outside before 'instructing' him in social etiquette as demanded by the seated Russian.

Six pairs of eyes watched every step he made as he had the temerity to approach Mr Ciesciu directly while he was eating. Surely, it would be easier to attempt to take a piece of meat from a hungry tiger. The four minders shot to their feet and stood either side of their benefactor.

"Mr Ciesciu, might I have a minute of your time?"

The proprietor now recognised the foolish young man to definitely be English. Each word had condemned him and sadly his actions would probably do even more damage before the next half hour had passed.

The oligarch didn't look up. His food was far more interesting than this stupid man, who would be nursing a broken arm long before he'd finished his current mouthful. There was a lengthy pause while he assessed exactly what the punishment should be. During this time the interloper was held in the steely gaze of the four minders who looked as though they were about to tear him limb from limb given just a snap of his fingers from their boss. Mr Ciesciu decided that he was going to play with this stupid and brazen boy who'd strayed into very treacherous waters.

"If you don't tell me something that is of interest to me in the next thirty seconds, then I assure you, that you'll have great difficulty in talking with a smashed jaw." He laughed as he continued to stare at his plate of food. The minders also laughed, and each now stepped forwards, preparing to administer said punishment in quadruplicate on the hapless buffoon.

"In that case, I have some files here." The young man fell over some of his speech as pressure mounted; doing his best to spit all the words out that he'd prepared. His forehead had broken out into a profuse sweat and his legs were shaking so much that the linen trousers were following in a perfect complementary rhythm.

"Someone claiming to be an associate of yours has befriended Alexis Mayberry."

Before he could say more the Russian interrupted him, "I don't know her and I don't have any associates, only people who I crush with my little finger, and those who do my bidding." A stumpy right wrist, sporting a vulgar bright gold Rolex, festooned with diamonds, appeared as he extended it in order to click his fingers to add effect.

The four minders grinned a little with anticipation. One cracked each of his knuckles in turn, because he had a feeling that his fists would be called into play any moment now. Looking at the visitor, he knew that the bony, thin-jawed man would not take much punishment. In point of fact he'd be screaming like a girl as soon as they'd grabbed him. The minder had had plenty of experience to know which body types would require more given force in order to administer a level of punishment. This sweating kid would require very little to maim him. He smiled a grisly smile as he remembered, happy day, that it was his turn to be allowed to strike the first few punches.

"Why should this woman, this whore, be of interest to me?"

"Well, I'm sure you've heard of Bollington glass."

The young man knew that everyone had heard of Bollington glass as it had recently been splashed across all the financial pages, given the recent breakthrough made by the company.

"No, never!" came from the oligarch, lying. Moreover, there was the shortest of fleeting glances now aimed in the young man's direction, as this single word, had probably saved him that day – 'Bollington'.

The visitor's furiously working mind thought that this was very strange as the company had also been recently promoted into the FTSE 100 reflecting its higher value, its share price having risen strongly of late.

"Why should I be interested in a company I've never heard of?"

The young man continued to sweat, and to make matters worse, his right leg was trembling uncontrollably while the left felt as if it were about to give way, and he dared not even think about the squealing from his bladder as he stood there in increasing discomfort. Trying to calm his legs only seemed to make his bladder more restless.

The oligarch chose this moment to scrutinise him in more detail, looking up from his meal for the first time. The four minders looked hungrily at him like a pack of rabid attack dogs, waiting to fall on their cornered prey.

Sensing that more evidence was going to be needed, and soon, the visitor pressed the dark panels of the case he carried. His fingerprints were scanned in the time it took a bead of sweat to run down the side of his forehead and on to his open-necked shirt. From the elegant case he withdrew two slim files.

One was a bulletin about Bollington glass, having perfected a new product called 'PV-Glass'. This was a glass panel capable of generating electricity as soon as light fell upon it. The panes were double-glazed and contained within the 'sandwich', a special dielectric, which when used as a spacer could then generate electricity. Such glazing had a slight reflective appearance and was ideal for replacing the glass cladding of skyscrapers. Having been in development for some time, the company announced that they had solved the technical problems of poor performance and the tendency to become cloudy with use. One large order had already been placed for a new prestige building in London. Furthermore, all accounts held that the order book was filling rapidly.

No sooner had the breakthrough been announced, and the company stock had been in big demand, with a corresponding rise in the share price. One hedge fund manager had bid for a ten million pound purchase of shares, but only received a fraction of the stock he'd wanted. Because the shares were very illiquid, the price had been driven even higher. Patent filings had been made across the globe in order to protect Bollington's intellectual property, pending an imminent worldwide rollout.

The other file, which contained information about Alexis Mayberry and Toby Richmond, remained unopened on the table.

The oligarch threw one of the files to the floor with an almost casual display of his annoyance. He did not reveal that he knew far more than could possibly be contained in such a thin file.

Moreover, his temper and the outrage that he feigned on his face was a very useful tool for hiding the fact that he sensed an excellent opportunity was now opening for him. The last thing he wanted to display was even a hint of excitement, which he recognised as something that would always betray an investor who was seeking to secure the best possible price for just about anything.

Of still greater significance was his understanding, backed by years of experience, that people always responded best to threats. The more graphic and violent the threat, especially when delivered quietly, with no trace of emotion, the better, and the sooner results were available to him.

"You'd better have something more useful than this, and soon, as I can feel indigestion coming on. Getting indigestion always makes me angry. My boys hate it when I get angry because I forget to pay them. If this happens, then, I'm afraid they will take it out on you. The last person who did this is still in hospital. Oh, no, sorry, I believe he is no longer a patient." The little laugh he gave out more than hinted at his true fate.

The waiter had chosen this minute to top up his customer's already generous glass of wine, in accordance with his boss' detailed instructions. Deciding, in the nick of time that now was an inopportune moment; he beat a hasty retreat as soon as he gauged the charged atmosphere in the room that even the air-conditioning could not cool.

The interloper now had the look resembling that of a baby impala that had strayed into a pride of five lions, each looking more hungry than the other, as he scanned the faces in front of him.

"The person passing himself off as your associate has befriended Alexis Mayberry." The young man took a calculated risk in repeating himself, hoping that it might focus the Russian's mind on the next part of the information. He pointed at the file, which remained on the table but had to withdraw his hand quickly as he could feel the tremor spreading upwards from his leg. He could only hope that he did not grow bored as a result. "We believe his interest is because she has 15% of the shares in Bollington glass, which is her father's company. Anyone who acquired these shares could demand a seat on the board or use it as a springboard to mount a hostile takeover. He plans to seduce her and take control of that stake."

"And you bring this to me, because?"

"Well, discerning, powerful and rich," he began, sensing that as many compliments as he could fit in were required at this point if he were to retain his teeth, "investors, like yourself are always on the lookout for unique and rare business opportunities, like the one we believe we have uncovered now. We then approach certain motivated and influential businessmen, who may find such information to be of use to them."

"Ah, and I take it, you then charge for this information?"
"Oh yes, indeed," the young man said naively. "Yes, we have a finder's fee. Our research is very comprehensive," he offered, doing his best to summon some enthusiasm from the Russian's face, which was still held in a forbidding rictus.

"And how much is this finder's fee?"

"Typically from fifteen thousand pounds, sterling."

"Ah sterling, yes, good old sterling." He laughed now almost hysterically. "Well, suppose I give you something much, much more valuable than 15,000 pounds, sterling: an offer that will be available to you for the next thirty seconds, when a very different offer will be the only one available to you." His men laughed now, too, for they had seen him make this generous bargain many times before. Usually it required them to get involved within seconds if the stranger was a bit slow off the mark. It was a mistake they'd be unlikely to ever make again.

"Suppose I allow you use of unbroken legs, that you can use to get out of here and never, ever interrupt my lunch again."

The young man's mouth opened but he decided that further speech would be unwise. Stretching out his hand, he attempted to retrieve the file, which lay on the table. The oligarch stabbed at it violently with his fork narrowly missing his fingers. Retrieving his still intact limb as quickly as shock and reflexes would allow, he looked more relieved than disappointed. By leaving now, then, hopefully, he would indeed still have use of his arms and his legs.

"Leave the paperwork, and also leave that cheap metal case you have there. You may go," was said almost graciously.

"Yes, yes of course."

Looking back at the file on the table, he hoped to distract the Russian. He handed over the case, but not before deftly closing it, and then fought to keep his face completely neutral with a tinge of fear. In so doing he managed to distract the odious man, while the triple spiral locks engaged with a slight whirr that his words had masked nicely. He angled the top surface away from the oligarch so that he could not see the flash from the panels as the 'locked' symbol appeared. Quickly doing an about turn, he left the restaurant as the four large, muscular and intimidating minders sneered at him with distaste. Leaving as quickly as his still trembling legs would carry him; he headed back towards the castle where a car waited for him. Within seconds the engine was revved without restraint and the occupants were on their way to Nicosia.

As he left, the pent-up atmosphere inside the restaurant was discharged almost as if a lightning bolt had brought a deluge of rain to clear the air. The oligarch took a deep mouthful, as if he were using mouthwash, of the red wine, which was the best that the restaurant, if not the whole of Kyrenia or even the entire Turkish Northern Cyprus, for that matter, had to offer.

He loved doing business with the English. He'd been hoping that the young man was going to wet himself. Courtesy of the slack jawed, weak bellied, spineless Englishman, he now had some vital information that he'd been avidly searching for, but in vain, for months. He glanced at the gorgeous case. He would look more closely at this later, which was a great mercy to the proprietor of the restaurant, if not to all those who would be on his yacht when he attempted to do so. He turned to his men, glowing with the bargain he'd won.

"Yes, this is a very big deal, without doubt. I have been looking for a way in. Once I have the bitch's 15%, the company will fall like a gift from the gods into my palm." He rubbed his palm for more effect.

"Get Vasiliy on the phone, now! Then, give him the details of this pair – tell him we will organise our very own takeover. I think this imposter will be our starting point, and though he does not know it yet, he will be helping us. Bring the launch round, we sail immediately and have my jet prepared. We fly to London within the hour. Tell Vasiliy to bring all that he has and we will compare our files whilst we are in the air."

Chapter XII

Shooter

Alexis had waited all afternoon. She was primed and ready with a million questions about her elusive contact, who'd been due to fly into Gatwick several hours before. In many ways she wasn't surprised; she'd obviously been played for some reason. Try as she might, however, she could neither fathom why she'd been the target, nor was she able to understand for what ulterior motive.

The other puzzle was the black credit card, for without doubt, they'd put within her hands massive riches, if she'd chosen to use it. Having gained the feeling that she could buy almost anything with that card, she was of the view that it would require unimaginable largesse before it would run out of what seemed like inexhaustible power.

No doubt he'd got cold feet, perhaps he knew that it was only a matter of time before someone would see through his delicate and colourful deception and guess that there was absolutely nothing of any substance behind that façade. It was like one of those film sets where the actor accidentally popped his hand through the castle wall or moved an unbelievably heavy object in such a way that everyone could tell it was made from polystyrene. A handsome face, perhaps, but certainly with no substance. She hated such people, now doubting that he would contact her.

Alexis then found Mr Forsythe's card. She wondered, too, if he would still be available. This she thought unlikely. The most alarming thing was her starting point. This, above all, was the only thing that she recognised and it had been her reason for getting involved in this sorry deception at the start. Someone had been buying shares in her company, and continued to do so.

Suddenly, she looked up to see a tall, striking woman with a well-honed physique standing in front of her.

"Alexis?"

"Yes that's me. Can I help you? And how did you get in unnoticed?"

"Forgive me, I slipped in while your secretary was distracted."

Alexis' spine was now tingling, sensing that there was something unusual, far from run-of-the-mill, about this woman who had suddenly appeared. She also sensed that she knew one or two of the answers that she'd been seeking, if not all of them. Wondering, with some concern, just how such a thing as a distraction could be possible, she started craning her neck round to see if her secretary was still at her desk, just outside the door. Looking at the phone, she considered phoning her to make sure she was all right.

Detecting her thoughts the visitor, continued, "Your secretary, Miss Davis, is quite safe, I can assure you." She added, "I am here to talk about Toby Richmond."

"Indeed, I was just thinking about him. I didn't expect him, or anyone else for that matter to show up. I see through your charade that, I am guessing, you're are part of?"

Her visitor ignored the inquisitive tones in the businesswoman's speech and continued, straight to the point, "I represent the Serious Fraud Office. Toby is a colleague of mine, and so is the man you met at our offices, Mr Forsythe. I need your help. The man we have been investigating has kidnapped Toby. You will know this man as Mr Ciesciu and you may also know that he is a disagreeable character. Toby was extracted at Gatwick Airport, and has not been heard from since yesterday. We have received a message this morning to say that he is being held and that his kidnappers, whom we believe are Mr Ciesciu and a team of paid thugs, will only negotiate with you and nobody else."

"Why is that, Miss, whatever your name is? What part do I play in all this? This has nothing to do with me. I can see that there is some sort of confidence trick at work but I am not sure why. I must look incredibly stupid and gullible, but I can say that I want nothing to do with anything you are offering. Please leave, leave now and leave me in peace. If you don't, then I'll phone the police and you can do some of your explaining to them, from a prison cell, together with lots more guff, no doubt. Just one thing before you go. That card you gave me, surely, it must be a financial scam of some sort. I do all the spending and somehow you cream off the money?"

"No, Miss Mayberry, I can reveal that it has nothing to do with money and I can assure you that no harm was supposed to come to you at any time."

"Meaning what, exactly?"

"Look, I can see that you have a great many questions and I promise that there will be time to answer every one of those questions to your heart's desire. For now time is pressing, however, and we only have a short window to recover him."

"And this is my problem?"

"I suspect by now you'll have realised that that card is a very rare and precious item. You could go out and buy a boat similar to the one you spent a few days on, with it and nobody would blink."

"And your point, here?"

"If we'd planned harm or to trick you in some way, we would have hardly left a card of that nature with you."

"Yes, I thought of that but I reckon this is the sweetener for a much bigger deal."

Her visitor smiled kindly, but more importantly, the young businesswoman impressed her.
"Time is pressing, Alexis, and I am afraid I must beg for your urgent help. I can offer you no possible reason why you should help us in this way, but I can reveal that if we do not respond to their demands, then they will most certainly kill him."

"Look, I'm not sure I believe any of this. I think my recent past has been based on a complete fabrication and I suspect this now. Please leave."

"I can assure you that they will kill him and that the stakes are very high."

"What are the stakes, exactly?" Alexis asked, her insightful line of questioning continuing to impress her visitor, who paused but, in that moment, realised she could go no further without revealing just a few more cards in the poor hand that she'd been dealt.

"The oligarch is after your share-holding in your father's company. He believes that by kidnapping Toby, he can put leverage on you to deal with him."

"So that's it. I should have known there is a bigger game in play and you had no interest in me whatsoever. Why should I help people who have lied and cheated in order to get to my father?"

"I can only promise that we will answer all your questions. I can assure you that neither money nor any influence in Bollington Glass is our motivating force and we will reveal more, in fact everything, to you once this is over." The visitor then played her trump card and she knew that one way or another events would either go with her or against her as soon as that card was played.

"Alexis, this is our chance to bring this man down. Neither your company nor your father's will be safe while he is out there. Too many influential people with too much money are backing him. But we now have a chance to strike. We can bring him down; you and others will benefit as a result. He is not used to taking 'no' for an answer and this has made him overstep the mark. We have the best opportunity in years to finish this and we need you. I need an answer, Alexis, because our plan needs to be enacted straight away. We believe he will be in a hurry to do the deal and then leave the country before the Home Office realise he is in England and before he revokes his offshore status. A man who is this wealthy simply cannot afford to linger on sovereign soil. I promise that if you help us, then you will receive a full explanation of what we have done and our motives."

"Very well, then, I will help, but in exchange I want to look Toby in the eye while he reveals to me exactly what is going on and why."

The tall woman held out her hand, "Yes, it's my promise."

"Here is a case," she handed over a beautiful attaché with its recessed hinge lines and the two dark panels on the top surface, machined from pure elemental aluminium. She continued, "These sensors will only respond to your prints and nobody else's. More information is inside and also a mobile phone, which Toby's kidnappers say they will use to contact you. I need you to read the contents of the files inside as soon as possible. Please keep the mobile with you at all times and inform me immediately when they place their demands. Two of my agents will arrive in one hour to collect you and we have prepared a rehearsal of the likely scenarios that you will be faced with. Our plan will be to keep you and Toby safe as a matter of priority, but we need to train you for every eventuality. There isn't much time. I'm afraid I cannot say that it isn't without risk to either him or you."

Looking at the beautiful case, Alexis stroked it with a flat palm, as it was perched on her lap. "I must say, you are very sure of yourself. Just how did you know I would agree to such foolhardy things?"

"I didn't, Miss Mayberry. I can only say that you were my last resort. Without your help, I dread to think what this man will do. I am sure you can see that me coming here was a mark of desperation. Please do not contact the police as the kidnappers have left instructions to say that if they show up they will harm him. I suspect that they will want you to present alone and they will use him as bait to get to you. For some reason the oligarch thinks you two are an item and that you will do anything to save him. He is hoping that he can exert leverage on you in this way."

"I can assure you, just as I will be Mr Ciesciu, when I set eyes on him, that nothing could be further from the truth. I agree to help you, but then, I am told everything, *everything* and then you, all of you, agree to leave me and my company alone."

"Yes, that is the deal I am authorised to make."

"Very well, then let's get on with it. I'll have read the material within the case by the time your men arrive."

"I have a feeling you'll be contacted very soon, probably today, which is another reason why we need to move quickly. Many thanks for speaking with me, Alexis. My colleagues will return for you as agreed."

Alexis looked at the case, marvelling at its svelte elegance. For sure, it was the most beautiful example she'd ever set eyes on. For a couple of minutes she sat there gently stroking its smooth, beautiful and flawless panels, but then remembered the job in hand and also that time was pressing. She lightly touched the dark sensors and the case opened without hesitation as her fingerprints were read instantly. She withdrew both the mobile phone and the paper files it contained. Setting the phone on the desk in front of her, she leaned back in her chair, placing her long legs also on the desk as she sat reading, deeply immersed in the information within.

The phone rang within the hour. Giving a little jump as it danced and hummed on the glass surface, she quickly reached for it to stop it from falling off the edge, noting that it had an unusual ring tone.

"Are you alone, Miss Mayberry?" The words came from the inanimate voice on the phone, having overtones of a deep Russian accent.

"Yes, I am."

"In that case, we have, your boyfriend, no? A man you know by the name of Toby. We plan to kill him if you do not do exactly as I say. Listen carefully to me now and we will let him go, provided you do as I am telling you now. We are looking for a stock transfer of your entire holding in Bollington glass. If you do not arrange for this immediately then we will kill him, no."

"I am not sure I can do that," she returned as calmly as she was able.

There was a long pause, while presumably, the person on the phone reported back to a third party.

"You have no choice. We will kill him, Miss Mayberry."

Refusing to be intimidated, she continued, "Surely, this is known as a 'deal under duress' and if you want my shares, which must be worth in excess of a 100 million pounds, then I am afraid you are going to have to agree a compromise with me. I am certainly not going to simply agree a stock transfer on the telephone. You could be anyone!"

The phone disconnected. Alexis set it down on the glass desk in front of her. She'd always tried to live her life in a bright and friendly manner, something that was noted by all she met. 'Sunlit uplands' was a phrase that she often used, if only to herself. She accepted it was an expression used by Winston Churchill in a slightly different context, but it served her purposes to think of it in this way. It seemed, however, that many were planning to abuse her good nature to trick her, or to use her, and she'd had just about a belly full of this.

Knowing in those moments that it was high time for her to take charge, to drive events, she reasoned that being timid had no place. Furthermore, although she knew that for now, she had to assume that her female visitor was telling her the truth, she also recognised that the outturn of events was in no way her fault. Toby was being held captive for reasons that had little, if anything, to do with her. Although she'd do everything to help him and would, in addition, relish her opportunity to ask as many questions as she wanted, she would manage events, from this point on, in her favour and in a way that she saw fit. Upon gaining the information she sought, also the assurances of those who'd shown interest in her, she'd insist that she was to be left alone for good.

The phone rang again. Deliberately letting it ring for a while, she was not going to appear so desperate to speak with these men. She felt that it was time for them to do a little sweating. Eventually, she clicked the 'receive-call' button.

She decided not to wait for him to speak. "Look, if you want my shares, then I need to see him to make sure he is still alive. I want proof of life and I am not going to do anything at all until I have this. And I certainly won't be transferring any shares to you or anyone else until I have it. He could be dead for all I know." She heard the caller, who was a different person than the one who'd first called, trying to get a word in edgewise, but she continued, "I need to see him with my own eyes, then we can do a deal, but not unless and until I do. You take it or leave it, and the deal remains the same no matter how many times you put the phone down on me!"

A short delay then occurred. Alexis simply waited, being in no mood to make any effort to fill an uncomfortable silence with the unsavoury characters attempting to dictate events.
"It seems we are going to do it your way, Miss Mayberry. Any police and I promise you, he will die a painful death, as will

you if you try any funny business. I am not used to people telling me what to do. Be at the following address tomorrow at 10am and come alone. Bring your stock transfer passwords. As soon as the deal is done you can then leave with your boyfriend." He gave her the address. "Have you got that clearly? Don't be late."

"Boyfriend, he is not, I can assure you," she insisted, before terminating the call.

She then phoned the number she'd been given by the SFO and was told that two men would be over to collect her. They would go through their strategy for the following day.

The next morning, Alexis waited in her car clutching the mobile phone. She did not wait long. They gave her an address in North East London and assured her that she would be under observation throughout her whole journey. If she were being followed, then they would know. She'd been informed that if this proved to be the case then Toby would be killed.
Selecting drive from the automatic gearbox, she drove sedately to the location. The phone went off again.

"Ahead of you, there is a disused brewery. Please walk in through the front entrance."

Grabbing her handbag from the front seat, she then walked to the dilapidated doors and pushed them open. Allowing them to close behind her, she became aware of two men moving behind her and upon turning, she could see that they'd locked and bolted them.

She walked into a large open space. Presumably in days gone by this is where the brewing process took place. Reflexively she sniffed the air, but concluded that the fresh hops, yeast and other ingredients were long gone. Glazed roof lights provided natural illumination but these, and the rest of the building, had seen better days. There seated just in front of her was the man she knew to be Mr Ciesciu. Alexis had studied enough photos of him on the tablet that Mr Forsythe had given her and also images she had obtained from her own searches. He was surrounded by at least twenty minders and she could detect movement from behind her in the upper storey of the deserted brewery.

"Mr Ciesciu, I presume?" she began with excitement rather than fear now coursing through her.

"You are correct, Miss Mayberry."

"So, you've kidnapped someone just to get hold of 15% of shares in my father's company? Why don't you just buy them like everyone else?"

"Kidnap is such an ugly word. We only wanted to talk with you. But of course, we both know that shares in your father's company Bollington glass are very illiquid and can be secured only in small quantities and with great difficulty. I am planning something much more ambitious, and you are going to help me."

"Whatever spin you like to use, I can promise you that kidnapping and extortion are both illegal and if the police were involved, then you'd be in deep water."

"Come, come now, Miss Mayberry, another ugly word. Only in the UK are such things frowned upon. I can assure you that most of our activities are well clear of the UK, where the ends always justify the means, somehow. You English are so prissy about such things and we foreigners laugh at you while you English look for fair play. We have the deal done before breakfast and before you have even risen. Once we have your

15% we will use this as leverage on your father, on the other shareholders and the company. He won't know what's hit him until it's far too late."

"He will fight you every step of the way. He is a very wealthy man."

"I don't think so, Miss. His wealth is trifling compared to the money I have at my disposal. We have massive funds behind us, and we will be ready to apply them in an instant. This is one of the few things I like about you English: you have some of my favourite expressions and one in particular is, I believe, 'money maketh the man'."
"In fact, I think that is from the Bible and we English usually say '*manners* maketh the man'. I have another saying Mr Ciesciu, 'Actions speak louder than words'."

"Only poor people say those words, Miss Mayberry and those who have lost, or are about to lose everything."

She decided that the word play was getting her nowhere. Moreover, she had delayed for long enough. The tracking device she carried in her handbag would have by now allowed the enforcement agency, the police and the SFO teams to be in place.

She just needed to delay for a little while longer. "Where is Toby?"

"Ah, the handsome Mr Richmond, I was wondering when you were going to ask me about him. Before I send Igor to get him, however, I am afraid we are going to have to search you, Miss Mayberry."

Holding the large handbag away from her, she looked down. As she did so, she brought both arms away from her torso so that they extended perpendicularly. Alexis had picked her clothes with care and was wearing a close-fitting short skirt that was well above mid-thigh and also a tight top to match with a plunging 'v' shaped neckline that revealed her ample décolletage at its stunning best. Simply the act of bringing her arms out exaggerated the line of the chest and also tended to bring the hem of the skirt even higher. Suddenly, the tension in the room became even more charged, for at least twenty men swallowed very hard at this beautiful businesswoman making such a movement.

She looked up with a puzzled, playful look on her face. Bringing one elegant arm down, she tugged with her thumb at the loose belt, which encircled her slender waist. "I'm not sure that there could be a lot hidden, are you?"

One or two of the men laughed spontaneously at this point, whilst another of the men came forward enthusiastically. Sheer delight registered on his face as he approached her, with the intention of imposing a thorough and heavy-handed search on the attractive woman.

Mr Ciesciu barked out orders. "That won't be necessary, Leonid, go and get our guest with Igor."

A look of barely restrained disappointment cascaded over Leonid's face as he stopped in his tracks. A reluctant about turn followed, in order to go to the back of the brewery, and with his colleague, he escorted their prisoner from a disused office.

"I hope that you've brought your broker's details as we requested, and any passwords that we will need to carry out the transfer." The oligarch picked up his laptop so that he could make it ready to process the transaction without delay.

"Yes, of course," she advised, "it's all in the handbag." She held the bag up for their inspection and at all times she kept it in view as if its contents were now crucial. "My details and the passwords for the on-line brokerage service."

Then she saw him. He'd obviously not slept and looked very dishevelled from the rough handling he'd without doubt received. In addition his clothes were dirty and both hands were tied behind his back with wire that looked excruciatingly tight. He looked down at the floor and his gait was hesitant and unsteady. So much so, that the men who'd been sent to get him were half supporting and half dragging him.

"Toby, are you all right?" she asked with concern spreading across her face as she saw the poor state he was in. "I'll have you out of here soon," she confirmed with a reassuring confidence.

He nodded and as he looked up she noticed the bruising to the cheekbones, which also extended to the temples and around the eye-sockets.

"So as you can see, Miss, we have brought the hostage and now if you would be so kind as to carry out the transfer, we can have this settled in minutes."

"Of course, one should never search a lady nor look in a lady's handbag, and believe me, it's all in the handbag."

She toyed with the unusual scarf that had been wrapped around her neck. The material was a little thick and an unusual grey-green colour that was almost khaki.

She held out the handbag as far away from her as she could. All the men present that day assumed that she was simply giving them a final observation of her lissom, toned figure.

Only Toby, knew that she'd never do such a thing and prepared himself for, what he could only conclude was, the unexpected. She didn't disappoint. Simultaneously, with her free hand she slipped the scarf from around her neck

Looking at Toby directly, she screamed, *"Monsieur l'Aerostier, tomber sur la planche maintenant, et vite."*

She'd heard him speaking French the night they'd been ballooning. She knew that he would understand her instructions about getting on the floor quickly.

She dropped the handbag. Toby hit the floor at the same time. The impact caused the smoke grenades to activate immediately. The charges went up simultaneously. White phosphorous, reacted explosively while the bag disintegrated. As it did so, vast clouds of phosphorous pentoxide were given off. A dense white fog came forth that enveloped everything and everyone within seconds.

She grabbed the 'scarf' that had been around her neck. Whilst the men had been admiring her other attributes they'd failed to scrutinise either the handbag or the scarf, which she now flicked with her wrists to unroll it. She placed the smoke hood as it unravelled over her head and pulled the filter down to activate it.

At the same time charges that had been set around the main entrance door went off and the tactical team rushed in. Most wore infra-red vision equipment to enable them to see through the clouds of smoke, as well as gas masks to enable them to breathe. She was unable to see Toby but she knew that one member of the team would be charged with finding and assisting him: carrying a spare mask for him to use. Mercifully, much of the smoke rose in the still air of the old brewery and she'd been informed that it would be possible to breathe if one stayed on the floor.

A shot rang out and she heard a member of the SCO19 team hit the floor violently as he remarked that he'd been shot in the leg and that someone had taken his mask. The next second Alexis was grabbed from behind and through the mask, that he'd removed from the injured member of Special Forces, Mr Ciesciu shouted to her.

"I have a gun here, and I won't be shooting at one of those fine legs of yours but straight through your head. Now come with me and quickly."

He dragged her off through a side door. They left behind chaos where the oligarch's minders were being systematically rounded up and pushed against one of the walls with their hands held aloft. Every one of them was coughing violently. The swirls of gas that continued to be produced only magnified their confusion and distress.

"I think you have caused me far too much trouble already today, you stupid bitch. The only reason you are still alive is that I am hoping you have memorised all the information I will need. If you haven't, then, I might as well shoot you now. Where is your car?" His short, thick but strong fingers tugged violently at the smoke hood and then at her hair in order to control her movements. She could feel his hands shaking with rage.

She cried out in agony.

"It won't hurt nearly as much when you are dead," he laughed, then continued, "Now, lead the way to your car. I won't ask you again," as he rammed the barrel of the gun abruptly into the back of her neck. She recoiled, once again, with the pain.

He removed the gas mask he'd ripped from the firearms officer. Manhandling her out via the rear door, they came around the building in order to find her car, which she'd left at the front, but just before the old brewery.

She nodded to the red Evoque and informed him that the keys were inside.

"I am sure that a clever woman, like you, has memorised all the passwords to her brokerage account and we may yet have a deal, though, of course, I can no longer vouch for your safety. You will drive to a nearby airfield, where transport awaits me, and if you are able to tell me, at that point, what I need to know, I may just let you live."

Specialist Firearms Command, SCO19 snipers were positioned on the roof of the opposite building. Some had binoculars and others lay prone on the roof, behind sniper rifles, mounted on stabilising tripods.

The oligarch saw the sniper scopes glinting in the sunshine and pulled the by now terrified woman directly into the line of fire, as a human shield. He knew that English fair play would never allow the snipers to fire if there were any possibility of the hostage getting shot. He pushed her violently forwards and soon they would be protected by the red SUV. Once inside the vehicle he knew that he would be safe. They would never catch him in time and he'd make sure that his helicopter was ready to go. If need be, he would take her with him as a hostage and she could always be disposed of once he had the information he sought.

Observers and gun laying officers looked through the binoculars, feeding information to the snipers and also headquarters. Their microphones and earpieces constantly relayed instructions.

"Hostage is obscuring the target."

"Clean shot is not possible."

"Lethal force is not authorised."

"Gun teams stand down."

"Repeat, lethal force is not authorised, gun teams to stand down."

"Stand down, pending further instructions."

Just as they relaxed back from their positions, a young woman with auburn hair raced to the edge of the roof. She was carrying her own rifle, of highly polished metal, which gleamed in the sunshine. The way she handled both herself and her weapon led them to believe that she was not a stranger to an operation of this kind. Nor could they, under any circumstances, receive the impression that she were here by coincidence. They stared at each other nonplussed, wondering who this woman could possibly be.

Completely ignoring all the SCO19 officers, she quickly positioned herself, her body tense at first, like a leopard about to leap forth. She then relaxed as she made calculations for the distance and wind speed. The firearm officers were initially stunned, but then one of them ran towards her, standing by the side of her prone figure.

She adjusted the sight, ignoring him totally.

Taking just one bullet out of her pocket she wiped it with a little cloth, then kissed it before feeding it into the rifle utilising its single bolt action. The rifle would only take one round at a time in its chamber, but she knew unequivocally that there would only be time for one shot, which would either bring success – or, without doubt, signify the loss of the hostage.

She readied to finalise her shot. Her smooth cheek caressed the stock of the rifle, like the familiar kiss from a tender lover.

The officer screamed at her, "Lethal force is not authorised: stand down."

She did not look at him, but she shouted back as she pulled her cheek away from the rifle, "If you let him get away now, then we'll never catch him, and God knows what he'll do to her."

"Stand down. These are our orders!"

"Once he gets in that car it's all over. The SFO have been after him for years," she insisted, calmness but firmness co-existing in her voice.

"Stand down, immediately! Live rounds are not authorised."
"Look, son, if you've not got the balls for a shot then please stand aside," she offered, calmly which irritated the officer to a frenzy.

"We have our orders. We are required to let him go in case collateral damage occurs to the hostage."

He then withdrew his sidearm and took the safety off with a loud click. Pointing it straight at her, he gave his final instructions. "Stand back from your weapon! No further warning will be issued." His hands now shook with rage and also nervousness as he looked at this stunning woman lying there, sporting a short dress but addressing herself to an advanced sniper rifle, which could only be special equipment. He spoke quickly into his microphone for further instructions.

Now, she did look at him directly. "It's like this. I am going to shoot that bastard, and the only way you are going to stop me is to shoot *me*, so either go on and get on with it, or *shut up;* or I might just miss. And nothing upsets me more than missing a shot, so, quiet! Go and file your nails or pull someone over for speeding, but do it quietly – *please!*"

He delayed just long enough, presumably while he waited for further instructions to cover this unusual event of another, and unrecognised, sniper appearing. She composed herself for a shot, once again snuggling her cheek against the rifle and its awesome power – just waiting to be unleashed. There was very little that she could see of her target and to make matters worse Alexis was struggling in his firm embrace and against the pistol now pointed to her forehead, so that all who were present could clearly see it.

The shooter closed her eyes, but briefly, as if summoning the inner calm needed, both to bond with her rifle and its deadly payload, and also to synchronise her whole body with the action that was being asked of it. She took a deep inhalation that seemed to last an age. Although, initially, her pretty eyes stared wide, they soon narrowed, darkening, now with deadly intent, as the exhalation came. Finally, she squeezed the precision trigger with one smooth unfaltering movement.

The rifle fired and the bullet was on its way. Only a slight whooshing noise signified that the projectile was being dispatched, the sound reporting back after a palpable delay as it went off at twice its speed. She checked, perfectly and precisely, the slight but predictable kick from her weapon and continued to gaze through the sniperscope.

She'd aimed for his left arm but mercifully at the last second brought the sight just a little higher to direct the bullet at his outer collar bone. The trade-off here was a simple but important one. The armour piercing round would have shattered the upper arm. The shot she chose, however, caused less damage but it was a lot more painful and would also have the effect of totally disabling his left arm, the one he was using to restrain Alexis. The crucial advantage of this last minute choice was that the intense pain would make it impossible for him to fire on the terrified woman.

As intended, the armour-tipped shell disrupted the end of the clavicle. The pain was severe, causing him to lurch violently. Bony fragments were projected inwards and one of these punctured his left lung. The pneumothorax so created caused him now to gasp violently for breath. His left arm now hanging forward and by his side as the collarbone was no longer able to support it. He dropped his weapon instantly. Using his right arm, he supported the left that had been plunged into a nexus of pain, disability, breathlessness and disappointment.

Alexis managed to break free at this point and a couple of armed police surrounded the kidnapper as he clutched at his shoulder, still gasping for air.

Within seconds a combination of police cars, ambulances and black cars with flashing blue lights converged on this one spot as they rushed in to block the road completely.

Alexis saw one ambulance take away the officer who'd been shot in the leg and another which presumably took Toby away. A third ambulance waited for Mr Ciesciu who was being fitted with a sling and screaming with terror more than pain as a bemused paramedic looked on. An oxygen mask hissed at him as he sat there, failure running with fury in a particularly unhappy combination.

Stowing her rifle in the boot of her Jaguar, F-Type, she rushed over to speak with Alexis, who said, "Nice shot, I could have sworn I felt it rush by my left cheek, just before it hit him."

"Perhaps best not to think of such things," Miss Clancy offered, the concern written to her face.

"Are you all right, Alexis?" she asked solicitously.

"Yes, I'm a little shaken, but I am glad that this is all over. How is Toby?"

"Ah yes, Toby, he'll be fine. He's tougher than he looks and he's received much worse over the years. They will check him over in casualty and, no doubt, discharge him later. I will ask him to visit you tomorrow to complete our bargain."

"I'd be grateful for that," Alexis offered quietly.

"Thank you for all your help, Alexis, we could not have done it without you."

"I believe so," she offered, matter-of-factly. "Please remember, I am to be henceforth left alone."

"We understand. Goodbye, Alexis." Miss Clancy offered the young businesswoman her hand, which was firm, smooth and dry. Alexis considered it to be the perfect handshake, just like Toby's.

Chapter XIII

One True Thing

The following day, just after 9am, Alexis was sitting at her desk. She'd told herself that she was going to have a productive day, but in reality so many thoughts were still running round her brain, on an endless loop, that she was unable to concentrate on anything. She'd even hesitated coming to a decision whether she wanted tea or coffee, when her secretary asked her if she would care for a drink. Ultimately, she realised that her sense of anticipation was so strong that she just had to sit back, looking regularly at the clock on the wall, as she waited for the person she was expecting.

Mercifully, it wasn't long before Hilary, her secretary, returned and this time with a sense of urgency and excitement written to her face.

"There's an absolutely gorgeous hunk of a man out there who wonders if you'd have time to see him. How many days would you like me to clear your schedule for?"

Alexis smiled coolly, refusing to remain anything other than calm, but informed her that thirty minutes would probably be more than enough. She remained seated when Hilary showed him in. Before going back to her desk, she somehow managed to mouth the word 'gorgeous' to her boss, but behind the visitor's back.

"Thank you, Miss Davis," she said to her secretary, trying to inject more seriousness into the prevailing atmosphere.

Toby sat in the chair, facing the desk that Hilary had suggested. He said, "Thank you. Thank you Alexis for saving me."

"I hope that you are recovering nicely?" she asked concernedly, while she looked at the bruises and wrists that looked very sore.

"I am, thanks to you."

"That's my pleasure Toby. Perhaps we're even now. I feel that I am at last getting to the end of all this. So tell me Toby, here we are. Why me, Toby? What interest can I possibly be to so many people, with this elaborate web of deception that you seem to have spun around me?"

Initially she paused so as to give him time to answer each of her questions, however, she found so many queuing within her overawed and distressed brain, that she just had to continue to pose them.

"Tell me. *Toby*, is that your real name, or does it vary from person to person? I need you to look me in the eye and tell me what's going on here, because nothing is as it seems, and I am far from certain as to why I have been swept along in all this."

Though she was desperate to hear some explanation, her feelings were in turmoil, for suspicion now conflated with a sense of betrayal. Knowing that all the questions still ran like a spring tide, she knew that she would have no peace until she found out all she needed to know – and that, of course, was everything.

"Is it all about the money? Is this just a scam to gain the 15% of equity that I own in my father's company? If you'd have asked me, I would have gladly given it to you, all one-hundred million pounds worth, in exchange for the one tiny thing you denied me – honesty."

"No, I promise this has nothing to do with money or of tricking you out of your shares."

"This little scam, this pack of lies, this false construct must have cost a fortune. The black credit card alone, must be backed by some serious funds or *someone* who has massive leverage at the bank. I appreciate that you were after the Russian chap, but why was I involved when surely you had other means at your disposal? Was he buying my shares?"

"No, we were," the simple words, now exploding within her consciousness.

"And, Mr Forsythe?"

"Our man."

"The *Financial Times* reporter?"

"Our man, too."

The horrified look that now appeared on her face precluded speech. She then realised how comprehensive had been the betrayal, but she was yet to learn to what end.

"The Russian bloke was a peripheral part of the mission. We learned that he had an interest in Bollington Glass, but not specifically in you."

"So you mean, I was used. I was a pawn in a greater game, and I was deceived."

The words were so hard for her to even say. She sickeningly feared, above all, the answers to those questions she struggled with. Only her curiosity and a sense of outrage now fuelled her progress through such difficult territory.

"Yes," was the only word that would serve at that moment.

"Was I used to get to him? To bring him down, and if so, why wasn't I told? Then I could have made my own mind up, or simply told you all to *leave me alone*."

"No, he was an aside to the central mission."

"Very well then, what was the mission and why put on all this?" she flapped her arms a little to hint at the nebulous nature of recent events. "Surely, this smokescreen with these blatant lies." Once again, she tried to pause, but knew ultimately that none of her questions would wait a scintilla longer. "What was your mission?"

He froze, suddenly lost for words. She knew this was the single piece of information about which events had turned and she just had to know. If she only had one last question that she were able to pose in her life, this was it.

Her voice had dropped by a semitone. She was calmer now, because she realised here was the information she sought above all else. Here it was, absolutely journey's end. Looking steadily at him, her eyes burning like elemental cobalt that must surely have reached melting point.

"Tell me, what was your mission?" She sensed his reluctance. Reluctance could only mean that the brutal truth was an agonising millisecond away. She continued, "You promised, if I helped you in your rescue, you would tell me. You tell me, and *you tell me now*." Her voice was at first insistent and then more entreating. "Tell me, and tell me now. I *need* to hear the truth and I *deserve it* after what you've put me through. So, I will ask again – *what* was your mission?"

"*You.* You were the mission." Even as the words left his lips, like explosions going off in the gap between them, he knew he could no longer maintain eye contact. Moreover, she was right, she deserved the truth.

She now glared at him, the blue eyes almost boring into him to clarify what she sensed was at last some semblance of truth. She continued, "*Me?* The mission? Whatever do you mean?"

"We were retained to change your life."

"My *life?*"

"Whatever for?"

"We were retained to do a job. That's what we do."

Alexis paused as if the Earth's rotation had been suspended. For a minute, she frantically digested this new information. Unfortunately its acquisition only generated more questions – questions that caused more bedevilment. "So, let's be clear, you and your organisation are paid a fee, a fee for a job!" She paused as she clarified each point. "To interfere in other people's lives? Why me, and for what possible reason? Massive funds have been spent here, but why? How could you possibly make it pay? *Who could possibly* want to change my life?"

"We are retained by some very wealthy people."

"Oh no, my *father!* He put you up to all this didn't he?"

"Our clients are confidential."

Anger grew in tandem with the turmoil as she uncovered more of the unpalatable and disturbing truth.

"Don't give me that load of crap, you are not working for a newspaper now! *He* engaged you, using *massive* funds, to change my life.

"Tell me, Toby? What gave you the right, the arrogance to think you could or should re-write my life? Who were you to judge? With your borrowed balloons and rented boats. Were you hoping to sweep me off my feet, bedazzle me? Oh, the old girl has a boring life; we'll just tart it up for a week or two for her. It obviously lacks a big boat and a hot air balloon, and she'll be fine. Ooh, perhaps a speedboat ride? It's like a trip to Disney – only *that would have been a bit cheaper*. I see now, my Dad's making up for the absent father, the person who was never there for me. Perhaps, you should have just tossed me over the side; *now* that would've changed my life a bit!"

"Forgive me, we were simply hoping to show you that there was a lot more out there than work."

She looked away. It was always said that the truth hurt and she felt as if she'd surely been stabbed right through the heart. Everything she'd done, everything she'd built, the person she'd become, the pains and turmoil she'd come through in carving a responsible life out for herself – one that had hurt nobody – was suddenly judged by others, and found wanting. They, in turn, had suggested a replacement. A replacement life that involved nothing more than holidays in sunny and snowy places. A radical change but based on neither truth nor substance. It was almost as if a committee had sat, judged her, and everything she'd done and then erased that, inverting her whole existence along lines that they thought it should follow.

Everything she represented, for sure, her very essence, had been ripped out, so that others might then redraw it, totally. And that simply because they believed they knew better. For a moment anger was displaced by disappointment in herself. Disappointment deep inside that would in turn evolve into acute distress that would know no limit.

"How stupid I've been," she said quietly, as the pitiless truth continued to find ways to torture her.

"I'm sorry," he offered, but he knew as the words left his lips there were none that he could voice that could even begin to repair the destruction that coursed within her, like a beautiful ice sculpture that had been left to the mercy of unforgiving sunshine.

"No, it's not good enough, not nearly good enough."

Pain accompanied by a deluge of tears was only seconds away. She had to finish what she wanted to say and then insist that he leave. "It seems I was just a job sheet, a little project for you arrogant bastards. Was any of it true? Any of it? One tiny thing, can you tell me? Or was it *all* a web of lies?"

At first his silence was the only answer that he could give. This was the only thing, sensing that his words would hurt her even more. Eventually he decided that throughout it all, one thing reigned supreme, an inviolable truth amongst the lies. He should have known, however, that even voicing it here and now would destroy her.

"Yes, just one thing."

"Tell me!"

"Somewhere in the middle of all this I fell…"

She screamed, the cry more heart rending than the one she'd have voiced if she'd gone off the cliff the day they'd met. Something she ardently wished for in that moment. "No, don't you dare! Don't you dare say it," her voice was breaking, rising to a crescendo at that juncture as she screamed at him. But all was not yet said. "Don't you dare try to make it all-right. It's *not* all right. It will *never* be all right and more lies from you won't change that. You just add more insult to injury, twist the knife, why don't you." Tears waited for her, building with an urgency, ready to torment the cheerful businesswoman and dissolve her like a sandcastle before the tide. "Your tawdry attempts to bedazzle me with vainglorious displays of excess and largesse, when there was absolutely nothing behind them but pure deception. You see, even you don't know what's real any more. You have lied for so long, and to so many. Not only that, you don't know what's wrong from right, and even when you are lying to yourself. Just how did you think your lies were going to change my life? Do you think they will suddenly make it perfect – all peachy perhaps? At least, boring though it must, obviously, seem to you and to my father, it's my life and it's a life I was quite happy with. It contained truth and at least some rectitude, whilst yours has none. Absolutely, none!"

In all the words in all the sentences that passed between them that day the one little word remained the saddest of all – 'was'.

"I'm sorry if I've been unkind."

"Please go, and go now."

She turned away from him, not so much to treat him with dismissive disfavour but more in that moment to hide the unending depth of misery patently applied to her face and the illimitable tears that drenched it like a monsoon. He left, quietly, with no more words being said. For mere words were incapable of re-writing time, of undoing ill-thought actions, of re-structuring whole sentences that had been spoken and received: or erasing hurt that had been given free rein like a conflagration in dry tinder.

Moreover, in that minute she'd moved from someone who'd seen nothing, to the person who now saw everything – and all of it wracked her tortured mind without mercy. What caused her great pain was the realisation that they were right; her life *was* boring. Even worse than this however, she now knew, this is why he hadn't responded. The times she'd been up close, whispered to him and gazed at him. The times when his eyes burned with barely restrained desire. No doubt they had a rule about not seducing their clients: he'd been 'on mission' throughout. And she was clearly nothing more than a subject. Maybe the easiest way to break a heart was to show someone you didn't want theirs. Ultimately, it was this simple, but final, step that hit her with obliterative intensity.

The door was closed but the sobs were plainly audible from well beyond her room. Hilary, too, looked ghastly and wondered how such a handsome man could do such harm in such a short time to her wonderful boss. Perhaps it was because he was so handsome.

Maisie was also in attendance, having heard that a visitor had arrived. She paced like a squirrel in a shoebox for many minutes before knocking and coming in. Looking at Toby as he left, she didn't really know what to think. He certainly didn't look like a bad person. But, then again, she reminded herself, they never did. Her first instinct was to find her boss rather than wonder too much what might have transpired. She entered the room. Hugging the devastated woman seemed to create more tears in both of them.

"I don't know what's happened to you. I can't begin to find words to even somehow start to make it right. I can't imagine what they might have done to you and why; what *he's* done to you, and why. I can only tell you what a wonderful person you are, how me and Peter love working here, with you. What a kind and generous soul you've always been, with an amazing business."

Peter joined them at this point – his face, too, on the edge of so many tears. Maisie continued, "If you'd permit me, however. We've noticed a big change in you in the past couple of weeks. Something is present now, in you, that's not been there for some time. In fact has not been there for many years. Tell me to shut up if you don't want to hear any more, or just smack me on my head, but some of those changes seem like good ones."

"It was all fabrication and deception. They just lied to me."

"Forgive me for suddenly appearing all wise, here. I have not been hurt, like you, but I don't see that. Lies I am sure there were aplenty, but I detect a change, an astounding change, here, and it's new. There's something glowing in a cold and bleak night, and I cannot believe that is a lie – whichever questionable methods were used to create it. Shout at me if I'm talking out of turn or if you think I can't possibly know what I'm talking about." She looked at her boss, the tear-stained, puffy face that looked inflamed and sore.

"They basically tried to show me that my life contains nothing," Alexis, clarified.

"Ooh, how silly of them to suggest that. Your life contains more in one heartbeat than many lives do in an eternity. Perhaps they were only trying to suggest that there was room for a little more within it? Which is true for all of us, no doubt." Maisie paused, doing her best to repair what seemed irreparable. "Get yourself home, and maybe we'll see you in a few days, because, believe it or not, we have a business to run here."

Alexis grabbed her handbag, hugged Maisie and Peter, followed by Hilary, and left the office with no more words being spoken. The three remaining looked at each other, as a stunned silence fed by surprise and disbelief washed over them.

Rather than go straight home, she went to see her father.

"Well, Dad, someone's been spending a lot of money on these jokers who couldn't get wet at a pool party."

Sensing immediately how badly things had turned out, he looked crestfallen and suddenly much older than the man she recognised as the person she admired above any other. He looked at her face, which had been mercilessly persecuted by misery and an endless flow of tears.

"So, why did you think my life needed changing? Perhaps if you'd been there for me when Mum died, instead of burying yourself in your work and leaving me to get on with it. Where do you think I got the idea? Just throw yourself into work and it all goes away. Don't need to deal with stuff. Don't need to think or to feel. Just cover it all in a load of work, and then don't worry about the rest.

"Who do you think you are to try to re-write my life? And just when did you think, at what point would I guess, I'd notice that I was surrounded by a bunch of imposters, and one crazy Russian with a nasty temper? I should have let him have those shares, and I reckon he would have given you a run for your money. Perhaps it would have stopped you sticking your nose in your daughter's life. A bunch of strangers, people who used any means at their disposal apart from the truth."

"I've tried, my love. I invite you round, I suggest holidays with me and Diane."

"I appreciate Diane is your wife, Dad and I'm happy for you, but she tries to be something she can never be, and that's my Mum. I know you needed to move on. So, you decided if you couldn't change my life, you'd pay others to do it for you. How typical of you, Dad. Oh, spend a couple of million here and it surely can't go wrong. I can then sail off into the sunset with the new type of life that someone thought I both needed and wanted. Only it was all false, like a script in a film, and not a good film."

"My darling, *you weren't living*, just working."

"And I am now, eh Dad, is this what you wanted?"

"I thought it for the best. I'm sorry."

"That's the thing that hurts the most. I don't believe that thinking played any part of this. Oh, chuck a few quid at them and they'll soon sort her. It isn't your life; you don't get to judge it.
I'm not your little girl any more Dad, I'm thirty. I thought they were arrogant with their 'oh we'll just change this and lie about that', but you take it to a whole new level. At least they were just in it for the money."

"Ali, you weren't living and for a young woman it wasn't right. It has nothing to do with Diane and me. I know that you miss your Mother. I miss her, too. Burying yourself in work isn't the way to make it heal. I wanted them to show you some new experiences; to make your heart beat a little faster. To see the sun rise and the moon set."

"So, you opt out of your life after Mum dies. Then you find someone new, whilst I get on with mine and build a successful business from scratch. Then that's not enough for you? Most Dads would be proud of a daughter who did this."

"And I am, my love, but work is not enough - it's never enough. I asked them if they could just open your eyes to something else, so that you would not make the same mistakes that I made."

"Well, they certainly did that, Dad, and all of them bad ones, all of them lies."

"I'm sorry. Forgive me?"

"I'm not sure I can. I feel too hurt."

Somewhere after love, anger had stepped in and having done so, hatred flickered in the gap that formed. It was to be some time before each would learn which would flourish in the coming days.

She walked away. He did not try to stop her, sensing that her anger was all-consuming in that moment.

After going straight home, she sat in silence for a couple of hours while her life imploded around her. So many thoughts now rushed through her brain, many of which were unsettling and uncomfortable.

Chapter XIV

Springtime in Vevey

For a week she did nothing. She spent her time at home, and mostly in her bed. No calls were answered, no TV was watched, no emails were read, no texts and no mobile calls. It was almost as though she'd never existed. It was all over. Her dreams and her tears had told her so. She sensed a vacuum had opened in her life. For sure it must be a rotten life. So many had spent so much time, and her dad so much money, in demonstrating this to her. Perhaps it would be best if it were over, and it seemed that not eating or drinking, for a few days at least, was the solution. One or two callers came. After ringing the bell and getting no response, they resorted to peering in through the windows to see if there was any trace of life. The answer phone filled with messages and then couldn't retain any more. It reflected just how he felt inside. Her life had been erased and nothing had replaced it.

In the end, it was probably hunger that saved her. Though at first she'd told herself that she wasn't even remotely hungry and would be unlikely ever to be so again, after a few days something offered an opposing view. Upon finding little within the house to eat, certainly nothing fresh, there began the slightest flicker of a recovery.

One other crucial idea came to her at that time, as her brain, no doubt fed by all-encompassing thoughts that only hunger could induce, realised that she'd got what she wanted. Her company was safe; the oligarch had declared his intention to move against her if only to get to her father and though Toby and his peers had used this, the threat was real enough. The Russian's plans were dashed for good because he would surely be detained imminently courtesy of Her Majesty, despite his assurances of powerful and influential allies.

She told herself that, strangely, this is what she'd set out to do – keep her company safe and just get on with her work. Work that she loved, surely above and beyond all else. The following day she returned, to her co-workers' delight.

Maisie hugged her. "Welcome back, are you all right?"

Avoiding the question was associated with loss of eye contact, so she was grateful when Maisie changed tack. "Come on, we've a company to run here. We have so much going on that it'll keep your mind busy."

Peter arrived, and after asking how she was, immediately launched into work-related matters – sensing that this was what she needed at that point in time. "Look Alexis, I've got to go to the studio in Vevey. I'm afraid we've hit a problem with the sapphire glass. It sounds like really bad news. We've had one or two reports saying that it's fading in direct sunshine. The deep blue is being bleached by the sunshine and it sounds nasty. I need to know if it's the whole batch or a small sample. This could be a big setback for us if it's widespread. I'm sure I don't have to tell you."

"Very well then, in that case I'll go," came from his boss.

"Are you sure, it could mean aggro from customers and suppliers."

Returning just the slightest flicker of a depleted smile, she continued, "That's just the thing, then, to keep my mind focussed on work, so it will be perfect."

Springtime in Vevey

"You are the boss, so just let me know if there is anything you need," he offered.

She boarded the next flight to Geneva; then caught a train along the north shore of the lake. She arrived in Vevey the same afternoon. The studio was a large double-fronted exhibition room that demonstrated concepts in stained glass to personal callers, who preferred to see examples, rather than view and purchase online. It had a spacious but empty flat above and Alexis reasoned that this would be a perfect base for the near future. At least for a while, as she got to grips with, possibly, the most serious threat to her business she'd encountered, save for the Russian, since she began.

By happy coincidence, Vevey in spring was a wonderful place to be. The hustle and bustle in the centre and the beautiful shops that were to be found in the old town just inland from Lake Geneva, were a welcome and visceral change of environment. In addition, Vevey was a short drive away from the ski slopes, and skiing in spring was exhilarating, if one were prepared to rise early before afternoon sun made the runs slushy. She was soon immersed in her work and spent days tracking down the problem with the sapphire glass. Mercifully, it was confined to a small batch, and although customers had to be mollified, the fact that the Chief Executive Officer of the company was personally involved, at the very least, assured them that it was being dealt with at the highest level.

Kurt Müller entered the studio a few days after Alexis had arrived. He spoke with Mirreille, one of the assistants who worked in the studio.

"Ah, Mr Müller, is everything all right?" She asked, responding to the worried look on his face.

"No, Mirreille, I had my wonderful stained glass window installed about a month ago. As you may remember it is south-facing, and tends to receive sun for much of the day. I am worried however, that parts of the window, what you refer to as the sapphire-blue areas, are steadily losing their colour. I am worried in case they are being damaged by the sunshine."

Alexis picked up on the conversation, approached and stood next to her assistant. "Hello, Mr Müller, I am Alexis Mayberry, CEO of the company. I am sorry you have been having problems. There have been concerns with a small batch of the blue glass we have used. We will do all that we can to rectify things for you. When would be a good time for me to come and take a look?"

The customer froze in his tracks, not prepared for the rapid response and at such a senior level. Only his smile betrayed him. "Miss Mayberry, I am speechless. Why, whenever would be convenient for you?"

"I have an hour now, Mr Müller. Would it be suitable for you?"

"Why yes, would you care to accompany me home and I will bring you back here as soon as you have taken a look? Please call me Kurt."

Alexis grabbed a small plastic box containing the equipment she needed and followed him out to his car. She entered the large black BMW by the passenger door and they soon arrived at his house, which was a newly built, very large residence on the outskirts of Vevey. It was constructed from hard woods and incorporated extensive glazed areas. There, to one end of the sitting room was a magnificent stained glass window extending to a height of three metres.

Springtime in Vevey

Alexis could see that the sapphire glass had been used higher up the glazed areas than she could reach.

"Kurt, I wonder if I could trouble you for a pair of stepladders?"

He soon returned with the ladders. She caught him surveying her legs with more than a passing interest, as she ascended the steps, but she decided, nevertheless, to press on with her examination of the suspect areas. Holding up the portable colorimeter she'd brought with her, within a few minutes she was able to give him her assessment.

"I am so sorry, Kurt. I have to tell you that your glass is from the faulty batch. Results of the tests with the colorimeter show, that the sun has definitely damaged the blue glass segments. I can tell you that it won't get any worse, but then again, it won't improve, either.

"Please accept my apologies. We will happily repair the entire panel, at no cost to you. If you prefer we can arrange compensation, and I can say that we would be prepared to reimburse the full cost. It's a very impressive window and we will work tirelessly until such time as you are happy with your purchase. Whichever you would prefer. If you would like us to repair it, then of course we would need to install temporary glazing while we remove this window, in order to work on it."

"Alexis, you have made me a very generous offer. In truth, I am very happy with it as it is and as long as it will not fade further, then I am happy to keep it."

"Very well then, Kurt, I can reimburse you for the full cost."

"No, Alexis, you have been more than kind to look into the matter personally. I wonder if I might tempt you out to dinner tonight and perhaps the pleasure of your company will be more than enough reimbursement for me."

"Then, in that case, how can I refuse? I will buy you dinner with pleasure."

The handsome Swiss man looked admiringly upon her and also appeared very pleased with the bargain he'd struck.

At 8pm he picked her up from the studio just on the edge of the old town of Vevey. He waited, holding the passenger door open to the large BMW. Noticing a further appreciative glance at her long legs, she tucked them in the car and the front foot well. The table was prepared for them as they reached the restaurant. The maître d' obviously knew him very well and escorted them to one of the nicest tables, one that had been reserved, in the packed restaurant.

"So Alexis, who do I have to thank for bringing you to Vevey?"

"Well, as you know, we opened the studio some six months ago. We became aware of concerns with a sample of the blue glass. As my colleagues are always telling me that I am under their feet, I volunteered to relocate here for a short time until we had settled the uncertainties with the faulty batch."

"Ah yes, I am delighted with my fading glass."

"Why is that, Kurt?"

"If it hadn't been for that window, then I would never have met you."

She looked at the blond hair, closely cut, which presented his hazel eyes and firm, raised cheekbones to maximum effect. She smiled and couldn't help but notice that his eyes dilated to their maximum aperture as she did so. The candlelight flickering in the semi-darkness as they looked at each other.

"Why, I am flattered, Kurt."

"No, Alexis you flatter me with your company. Are you planning to stay in Vevey much longer?"

"No, in truth my work here is almost finished, and we have repaired or compensated, mercifully, all those who have cause for complaint."

"Then perhaps, I should have asked for a replacement to persuade you to stay a little longer."

"My team will still be happy to do this, if you so wish, Kurt?"

"No, I could not bear to part with the window that you touched."

Alexis smiled, but sensed that his interest in her was a little too enthusiastic. Whilst being pleased with the attention, she detected he was an intense man and it wasn't long before he told her that he'd recently been through a divorce. She estimated that he was in his mid-thirties and wondered if his tendency to be infatuated with someone, he'd only just met, hid an obsessive nature. Her first instincts were unfortunately correct and he continued to shower her with compliments for the whole evening.

In addition, whenever she looked at him, she found the hazel eyes staring back at her unwaveringly. Even worse than all these things, however, was the way he leant forwards over the table so as to attempt to get much closer than politeness dictated. In addition there was the fact that his knee kept brushing her leg under the table. At first she considered that this was a simple accident and that perhaps the tables were a little small. But when it happened on a further two occasions and each episode seemed to linger for what felt like an eternity, then she knew she was in trouble. He also took every available opportunity to grab and caress her hand or her arm, whatever part of her body remained within reducing range as he leaned ever closer.

Sadly, what started out as a pleasant evening in prospect became just a little too claustrophobic for her liking and she was pleased when they'd finished their coffee and she was able to motion for the bill. Despite their agreement he appeared desperate to settle it, but she insisted, thinking that this was now the wisest course of action. More and more she was delighted that she'd told him that she'd be leaving soon. As soon as they found his car he asked her if she'd like to go back with him for coffee.

"Come back with me Alexis, and I can show you the window's beautiful colours in the evening."

"Thank you, Kurt, but I have to be up early tomorrow to meet the suppliers of the glass. They have agreed to some compensation for the defective panels," she declared firmly, keeping to herself that they were not due to arrive until midday. Realising that it was time to beat a hasty retreat from the handsome but intense man who was demonstrating more of his obsessive tendencies as time passed, she walked quickly back to his parked car – not wishing to linger with him on the streets with their subdued old-town lighting.

Thinking quickly, she made a sufficiently convincing case for her to return to the studio and it was with great reluctance that he drove her. As he stopped the car precipitously, he leant over to attempt to kiss her with more eagerness than she was comfortable with. He now placed his hot hand on her knee and it started to creep ever higher. She managed to vacate the car before she became embroiled in some desperate fumble, like a schoolgirl trapped behind the bike sheds by some pubescent boy dealing with his first crush. Mercifully, she was able to identify the door release catch and deftly opened the door in the nick of time so that she could slip through the opening.

As she thanked him for a wonderful evening, she stood with the passenger door between the two of them like a shield protecting her from the forces of evil. She took her time to speak to him via the open window. "So nice to have met you and please think about our offer to replace the glazing or reimburse you. I'll be leaving soon, back to England, but my offer remains and any of my staff will be pleased to assist you," she said with a business-like tone to her voice, as she stood, thankfully, outside the car.

Waving him off with some considerable relief, she thought of Mr Forsythe and said aloud to herself, "Now, *that* is unsafe in taxis!"

Making sure that the BMW had disappeared from sight; she then entered the studio and closed the door behind her before locking it securely. Over the next few days Mr Müller returned to the studios on four more occasions and telephoned a further six. Mirreille and the male staff were despatched to answer the phone and also to greet personal callers. When messages were left, he was told that their boss was either with clients or on a day's vacation.

*****

It was to be just over two weeks later that Miss Clancy entered the large studio just near the old town of Vevey. Alexis had been discussing with her Swiss team a refurbishment of the large premises, reflecting their full order book and significant demand.

She looked up briefly as Miss Clancy entered. Her heart sank and her bright mood collapsed as soon as she saw her. Her presence reminded her instantly of events and feelings that she was desperate to escape. Ultimately, she clung to the simple fact that there was nothing more to be said, or so she believed. Looking at her with calmness, bordering on disinterest, she said, "I thought you promised, you all promised, to leave me alone when it was all over."

"Yes, that's true. I am here more out of a measure of desperation."

"With you people it's always desperation. Go on then, you have thirty seconds, so talk fast." Alexis was in no way an unforgiving person, but she retained a deep distrust of the Horizon team and wondered if they were capable of sticking to their pledges. She accepted that her recovery had depended on re-engaging with the life she knew, one that was well away from them. Her father had given her reassurances that the mission was over, so at least this gave her some confidence. She waited patiently for the words that would follow from Miss Clancy.

"He's disappeared, seemingly off the face of the earth. He is not answering his calls, his phone has gone dead, not even giving off a signal, and nobody has seen a trace of him for over a week. Can I ask you, have you any idea where he might be?"

Alexis was just about to ask Miss Clancy how she thought she would possibly know, but seeing the worried look on her face, caused her to soften this stance, and the reply that queued within her consciousness.

Springtime in Vevey

"No, I am sorry. We are talking about *Toby*, I presume? I have had no contact with him since the day after the kidnap. He came to see me, as you promised me he would. I asked that this would be for the very last time and it seems he has stuck to his side of the bargain."

"Okay, it was a bit of a long shot, so to speak." The little smile appeared, but only briefly. "I am sorry to trouble you, and I will keep my promise. This will be the last time you'll see me."

"Very well, then. Goodbye." She held out her hand and almost turned towards the door.

"I've never seen him act like this, even when a mission goes wrong – though that's rare."

"I can only suggest that you should have thought of all of this. Seems like you've played with fire and you are about to get burned," concluded Alexis.

"I know, I did warn him that we should not take your case on. It was well outside our envelope, shall I say."

"So why did you? Was it simply for the money?"

Miss Clancy laughed. "No, I promise it wasn't that. Do you want to know why we took it on?"

Despite doing her best to pause for long enough to register her disinterest, Alexis was fired by curiosity as she eventually nodded to her visitor to continue.

"It was you!"

"Me! Don't blame me for a mess of your making. I was the victim here, of your poor planning and poor execution of an ill-conceived idea."

Miss Clancy knew that she just had to keep talking. "He'd agreed with me that we shouldn't touch the case. Then, for some stupid reason I put up some pictures, one of which was yours. In that moment, that second, he changed his mind."

"Oh no, don't try to tell me. This has nothing to do with me."

"He took one look and said he thought we should take it on."

"I don't know whether to be flattered or insulted. He ruined my life. He *nearly* ruined my life on a quick look at a snapshot!"

"I'd be flattered, if I were you, Alexis. Within thirty seconds he said 'let's do it', and here we are."

"It has *nothing* to do with me. Please don't try to pin this train wreck, this debacle, or this fiasco on me. As I believe I've said, I am the victim here, not the perpetrator, so please don't insult me by roping me in to this farrago of lies," she offered as adamantly as politeness and the struggle for inner calm would allow. She kept telling herself 'sunlit uplands', 'sunlit uplands', as she spoke.

"You thought we did this for the money? Money motivates some, but that's not who we are. Toby set up our operation ten years ago. I was his first recruit. His family were very wealthy. I knew when the Russian abducted him that he would have a very hard time of it. We've been following Mr Ciesciu for some time and we'd received ample information about his ruthlessness and brutality. I should have insisted that we pull out before this point; there and then, but he would not hear of it. He insisted we go forward.

"Nearly twelve years ago, his Mum and sister were kidnapped for a ransom of a million pounds. His father got the money together in an instant, and said he wanted to pay. The police said that he was not to. They would negotiate and act as brokers. It was fine for them to say that, it wasn't their Mum or their sister.

"Toby's Dad was going to do the money drop, but the police intervened, made a real hash of it and in the ensuing mayhem, they were both killed." Miss Clancy clicked her long fingers, as if the last light in the world had just been extinguished.

"His father blamed himself. He thought it looked as though he didn't want to pay. He never got over the guilt. He committed suicide a short time later by jumping off a motorway bridge. Toby was not quite nineteen. He set up Horizon the following year, saying that he did not want other families to go through what he'd been through.

"Pitiable rich folk, who is going to grieve for them? People detest and despise them, and certainly nobody wants to see things from their perspective, or the problems they face. Everyone sucks up to them when it suits them and use or prey off them. It's not very trendy to have sympathy for the mega rich. For sure, it's easier to feel jealousy and resentment toward them. Yet they often have more than their fair share of heartaches. This is what Toby set out to try and resolve.

"I know it's not usual to think of rich people in this way. Who cares? They even loathe each other and there is a certain schadenfreude when something happens to one of their number. So called 'friends' and colleagues will, as likely as not, see it as an opportunity to beat them socially or in business, to step over them – or to just gloat at their misfortune. The more colourful their undoing, the better.

"Toby isn't like that. He sees the tortured souls, the wayward children, the drugs and alcohol, the rich people with absolutely no one around them who can be trusted. As often as not, these wealthy types don't even have anyone with an ounce of gumption or common sense. Much worse, without doubt, are their families, wives or husbands who have torrid affairs while their spouse is working their socks off, or kids who don't see the point in it all, drop out at everything and then spend millions in a few months, on nothing!

"This is the eternal dilemma for the talented rich person; they rarely reproduce themselves. Whether they cut their kids off, or lavish expense accounts on them, it doesn't change the outcome – their lives still go down the toilet. Then, of course, there are the tricksters, those who seek to relieve them of a few bob. Not forgetting the newspapers. Newsmen love rich people. They love the glossy photos they generate before some exotic backdrop. They thirst for their exorbitant lifestyle, sought after by many, but acquired by few. They live for exposing their little peccadillos, or showing them with their trousers down, quite literally. Even when they fail to grab a suitable story, they publish hyped-up reports of their mistakes and their misdeeds – oh, and along the way, they sell a few newspapers for their owners, some other very rich person who laughs all the way to the bank at the misfortune of his peers.

"They all do their bit to degrade and destroy the wealthy who have enough disasters of their own making. Who is going to worry about that? Well, believe it or not, he does and he tries his best where he can, and when he can, to fix it, one case at a time. Our job was to help out, case-by-case, mission-by-mission. To run those missions, plot the outcomes, the prevailing situation and calculate the probability figures at each fork in the road and come up with the most likely scenario. You may believe that he lied to you, and I can see why. He'd never want to hurt you or anyone else. That boat, that yacht and that balloon are all his. He once told me that without people in his life to share them with, they don't mean a great deal. This is *why* he does what he does. That's just *what* he does and what he's *always* done until now – something's different this time and I believe I know why."

Alexis listened with amazement. Without doubt, she'd seen some tawdry confidence trick that had been ill thought, and hence had gone badly awry. She'd never grasped that there might just be a more complex, more detailed picture – until now. Remaining silent, she realised that Miss Clancy was about to reveal something momentous.

"He's in love with you. And I think I knew the moment when it happened. Call me crazy, but I think it happened the second I put your picture up, and frankly, I can see why, too. I know all about men, their foibles, their strengths and their many weaknesses. I see the way they look, some glance, some stare. The tales they tell and their little tricks to get you where they want you, but I've never seen him or indeed any man look at me the way I saw him look at your photo! This is a shame for me, because *I think he should be in love with me*. I've worked with him for ten years. The things we've shared and the wonderful projects we've undertaken, together. I can tell you see us as a team of 'no-hopers', but trust me; it's a rare thing that we fail. In fact, we've run some fantastic missions and losing isn't an option, believe it or not.

"I've been in love with him since the day I met him. Heaven knows I have dropped enough hints. I look at him all doe-eyes, I get close, sometimes really close. On occasion, I even hug him and kiss him and he does the same to me. The length of time we've known each other and the hours we've worked. Only, when he hugs me, he acts like it's his younger sister, and yet, when I get hold of him, well, let's just say, I want to *really* get hold of him. Then I tried the tight top. I leant over him brushing against him. I moved on to the plunging neckline – not a flicker. I then tried the tight pencil skirt, the short skirt and even a very nice skater skirt I have – didn't even notice. I've resorted to a few tears; he pats my knee like I'm a golden retriever.

"I've also flaunted the high, spiky heels and he asked me if I get bunions from wearing them. One day I even came in wearing seamed stockings, a suspender belt and a slit skirt, they nearly killed me. He asked me if I was going to a fancy dress!"

"That happened to me, bought them for my boyfriend, came home early one day and found him wearing them!" Alexis interjected.

"Ouch! That's not so good. So, Alexis, you can see that I am hoping that you'll tell me in a minute that you don't want him and that you'll *never* want him. If I'm able to tell him that then maybe I'll just have a chance. I used to think that he was gay, not that that's a concern for me. Nor is him looking at me like I guess he used to look at his younger sister – I could live with that. Then, I saw the way he looked at you, or at your picture, I should say. And I knew, there and then, the fire was burning – but it needs different fuel. This is why I'm searching for him – to tell him as soon as I can. I may just have a shot, so to speak, at catching him on the rebound."

She paused for minute not just to catch her breath but also to compose herself. She became aware that she'd perhaps given too much away.

"So Alexis, if I do find him, and I will find him, sooner or later, do you mind if I say that to him?"

"I am sorry Miss Clancy, I don't know where he is, and if I did I would tell you."

"That's all right, Alexis. I knew that you were my last resort, and I do apologise for going back on my promise. He really is the most wonderful man that I have ever known. I can see now, that I need to tell him that, and also to make him listen to me. Your disinterest will help me. If something has happened to him, then I don't know what I'll do. I am sorry, too, that we took on your mission, but at least it showed me something vital. I realise we only have ourselves to blame, but I suspect you will be our last mission, the final Horizon, if you will." Shaking her head as if she'd awoken from a trance, she looked towards the exit. "Forgive me, Alexis, I am going on here like a lovesick schoolgirl. I'll just say goodbye and go."

Alexis couldn't hear all that had been said without a response. Rushing forwards, she hugged Miss Clancy. For a moment Alexis thought that she could detect moisture in the corners of her eyes, but one blink later, and it was gone. One further blink and she was turning to the door.

"I'm sorry I could not have been more help," Alexis offered, as the other woman vacated the premises and walked towards the city centre.

Just before she did so, however, she glanced at Alexis, offering her an almost imperceptible nod. Alexis knew that Miss Clancy was not one for redundant and superfluous gestures, but thought no more about it. It was only deep in the night that she realised this was a sign that the vanquished might give the victor – the moment had now passed to Alexis.

That evening Alexis had a very disturbed night. However, somewhere between the hours of 3am and 4am she entered briefly what is known as rapid eye movement sleep, where dreams came to her. Upon awaking the following morning, she realised that she knew exactly where he would be. The picture she'd seen in the chalet was not the owner's family, it was his chalet and his family; he was the little boy, and the girl, his sister.

Chapter XV

Dragons' Breath

After a quick breakfast, Alexis jumped into her car and headed east. She drove as fast as driving conditions and the speed cameras would allow. Continuing throughout the morning, her car made a slow but steady climb and the outside temperature began to drop steadily. Although the sunshine continued to hold mastery over the day, no sooner had she left Lake Leman behind, than the green fields and fertile land took on a dusting of snow, which thickened steadily. She was glad of her softer winter tyres that performed beautifully on these cold, slushy conditions.

Not long after crossing into Austria, she reached Mayrhofen, the village where she'd first met Toby. This being the place he'd saved her and where he'd collected her that night, not that long ago, so that they could go hot air ballooning.

She retrieved her ski gear from the boot, having remembered to store it at the studio in Vevey. Studying the electronic board, which gave a summary of the condition of the runs and also how many were open, she looked with dismay as red lights flashed. An unusually warm spring had alternated with heavy overnight falls of snow, especially at higher altitudes. As she looked at the display, she could see that the blinking red indicators were spreading steadily, meaning that more and more pistes were being closed. This could only be because there was a significant risk of avalanches. The ski patrol would be very busy up on the mountain, bringing people off the slopes to safety.

Entering the ski-hire shop, she selected some all-mountain skis, which were a little wider than usual, as she knew she'd be skiing over thick and possibly drifting snow. She presented her boots so that the skis could be fitted into the bindings.

The attendant came over to her. "I am not sure you'll be able to get much skiing done today. They are closing the pistes as we speak. I very much doubt that many, if any, will remain open higher up the mountain and I certainly don't think you'll be able to use *these* today," he clarified as he pointed to the special skis. "There is a significant avalanche risk, and they are saying that the whole mountain is unstable."

Alexis nodded politely, but asked that he continue to fit them anyway. She now started moving with a sense of urgency, for she knew that any minute they'd close the lifts, not just the slopes. Lift closure would mean she'd be unable to get up there. Something told her that time was of the essence, but she did not know why. Possibly it was thoughts as to why he'd turned his phone off, for even in her darkest hour she'd kept hers switched on, even if she'd answered no calls.

In a flurry of movement, she grabbed a spare ski helmet, a rucksack that was filled with avalanche survival gear and a transponder. Then she asked the ski fitter to tighten the bindings as tight as he thought permissible – and to please hurry. She noticed an item of the very latest avalanche survival systems. This was a backpack that also contained an anti-avalanche air bag system. She'd read of them and their use, but never seen one before. Without a moment's hesitation, she immediately swapped the simple rucksack she'd initially chosen for this much more expensive one featuring the airbags.

Grabbing everything, she retrieved the black credit card and tossed it on to the counter before running with her equipment out of the hire-shop. It lay on the worktop as the attendant marvelled at its rare beauty.

Dashing over the road, she could see that the lift was still running, but, absolute disaster, it was being used purely to bring skiers down. Anyone wanting to go up the mountain was being turned away with a grave shake of the head from the attendant. She went through the side of the lift that conveyed people up to the slopes. The operator nearly didn't see her, as he was engrossed in getting as many down as quickly as possible.

"I am sorry, I can't let you go up there. We are bringing everyone down. It's too unstable," he began.

"My friend owns Chalet Rosa, and he says he'll be up there for days. He tells me he'll be so lonely. I will be very careful and keep well away from the ridge. I can't leave him up there on his own."

It was only when she patted the avalanche survival gear that he thought that she seemed to know what she was about. Provided she kept away from the unstable ridge, that they were hoping to blow with charges, she'd be fine. Looking nervously over his shoulder at his supervisor, he knew that he would never agree. He looked at the pretty girl again, now in an agony of indecision.

"Please, he's my boyfriend and he says he'll be stuck up there for days. I will be very, very, careful." The open, deep-blue eyes were now at their most entreating.

Swallowing hard under such an enticing vision, he then nodded, looking in the direction of his supervisor who was fully engaged bringing people down.

Alexis charged forward quickly into the upward bound side of the cable car taking her skis inside the cabin with her, but sat as low as possible, in case she was seen and the whole thing was halted. Upon reaching the top-station, she knew she'd have one more chair lift to take. This was also deserted, but still running.

She approached the operator, who said, "I'm just about to shut down. Nobody is up there; even the Ski Patrol say it's unsafe."

She tapped the bag as she spoke to him. "No, they are going to blast the ridge. They are waiting for these charges." He looked very puzzled, but he knew that if they were going to apply controlled explosions, then they would not want to be kept waiting, as any delay would endanger their lives and also that of many others into the bargain. "They have asked me to bring up some more charges, they are hoping to blow the whole mountain," she lied.

"In that case I'd better let you go up. Are you a member of the Ski Patrol? I haven't seen you before."

"Oh, they've sent me in from Zell. My expertise is detonating avalanches."

Suddenly, with neither further words nor hesitation, she'd jumped on the four-man lift and was in the process of being whisked to the top. Not even an attendant awaited her as she reached the exit gate. Within minutes of getting off the lift it was brought to a halt. The chairs now swung gently under the effects of the swirling breeze and the rapid stop that had been made by the operator, who was keen to get down to the village in order to leave the perilous work in the hands of the experts.

Spring, after intense periods of snowfall, was especially troublesome, as the peaks were pregnant with metre upon metre of snow. This froze solid at night only for it to thaw in the warmer days making it layer like a cake – except each 'layer' weighed thousands of tons.

Adding to the destructive potential of the situation was not simply the amount of snow but also its type. At this time of year the snowflakes were in the form of a flat disc shape, which was ideally suited to increase the instability in those layers. The slightest provocation was often all that would be required for the whole lot to come down. The immense destructive force sweeping everything in its wake, not stopping until every flake of precariously stacked snow had been jettisoned down the slope.

The situation called for experts to detonate precisely placed, controlled charges to deliberately bring down such unstable collections – provided that the slopes could be closed while they did so. It was a specialised and dangerous job and over the years had involved fatalities even amongst those who knew the terrain well.

Refusing to be outdone, a vicious but precisely directed wind swooped over the massif to add a deathly twist to the cataclysmic conditions. Blowing back over the top of the ridge towards them, this created an eddy on the lee side of the crest of the peak causing it to build up a gigantic overhang – in essence a ledge of unpredictable drifts. Experts maintained that man knew less about avalanches than the surface of the moon but even the mildly knowledgeable knew that conflated here were all the factors needed for the most violent and deadly type of avalanche – the dry slab avalanche. Furthermore, the conditions were too dangerous to risk any of the ski patrol. It was a much more prudent, safer decision to close the whole expanse in its entirety. Everyone still up there was heading down as fast as they could – Armageddon was upon them.

Coming off the four-man lift, Alexis skied down from the windward side of the left extreme edge of the crag where the covering of snow was much thinner and therefore more stable. Espying the chalet, she continued down with the rucksack on her back, carrying the spare helmet. The door was open and she called inside, but she knew even before she did so that he was not there. As she returned to the spot where she'd left her skis, she could see tracks heading off across the foothills of the mountain. Looking up at the peaks, she could not see him anywhere. She then plucked out the binoculars from her backpack and scanned the ridge on the other side of the valley.

Courtesy of the binoculars, she could now see just how menacing the overhang of snow was. Her mouth dried and her pulse fired as she finally realised how critical the situation. A million tons of snow was waiting for its chance to break off, like an icicle hanging from a roof, and to then continue downwards with Biblical force. Though the track would clearly miss the chalet, she could see that the valley would not escape and would be the main recipient of such a deluge. Absolute mayhem could be unleashed with the slightest provocation – and without warning.

Raising the binoculars again, she swept her field of view slightly further down the mountain – and, at last, she saw him. Using his poles in a frenzy of activity, he was attempting to cross the slope. Unfortunately, the drifts remained soft and the poles simply sank without providing a firm base to propel him forwards. To make matters worse he was crossing the relatively flat part of the saddle between peaks, thereby preventing him from skiing downward. All his strength was dissipating by his efforts in traversing the snowfield, now far too soft and too deep to allow any sort of progress and certainly not enough time to make the crossing if the unthinkable happened. She saw him looking up at the peaks wondering if he still had time to do so. Moreover, this, the deepest part of the valley, would give rise to the most violent part of the avalanche – a point from where nobody would survive.

She realised that he'd rejected driving the Ski-doo across the slope because its weight could easily trigger an avalanche. A skier's weight spread over two all-mountain skis represented the lowest density and therefore, one that was most likely to be successful in completing the crossing.

Alexis wondered in that moment, if only she could reach him in time. He was making such slow progress, following him would only gift the mountain two bodies. In addition, there was no gradient for her to ski across. Only effort-sapping and soul-destroying polling could move a skier forward through that deadly zone. She could see even from this distance that it would be foolhardy. She thought about taking her skis off and climbing up the extreme left edge of the mountain and then utilising the height advantage, she'd win to ski diagonally over to him. She reasoned that this would take too long. In any event her boots would soon sink in the deep powder, stalling any progress.

She looked again at the Ski-doo. He'd obviously toyed with the idea of taking it, but dismissed it as being too dangerous. Mercifully, however, he'd left the keys in. A daring plan formulated quickly within her agile brain. Slipping her skis off, she slotted them in the rail at the back of the tracked vehicle. She knew in that exact moment what she'd have to do to save him.

Alexis considered, once again, the extreme left ridge, which was an area that had been swept by the wind and would provide a firmer and more stable route. She would use this as a track for the Ski-doo to convey her directly up the mountain. Using the binoculars, she plotted the route of her ascent. The machine burst into life, but she deliberately operated the throttle with restraint, knowing that intense or loud noises could trigger an avalanche just as easily as asking it to bear too much weight. Driving along this approach, she hung on for as long as she could. After some considerable distance, the rear tread sank too far into the surface as the incline became too steep to make any further progress. The machine became increasingly disadvantaged by the angle of the slope, the depth of powder and its own weight. Dismounting, she made her final preparation to pluck him from the eye of an avalanche.

Firmly fastening the straps of her helmet, she also tightened the straps to the emergency backpack. She then clipped on her skis having to angle them perpendicularly across the steep piste. Using her poles to steady her until the job was done, she was ready to begin.

She set off. If anyone could cross an unstable field of snow, *it was she*. If anyone could reach him, *it was she*. She aimed straight for him, her track diagonally across the treacherous slope, pregnant with ton upon ton of snow.

Her progress was at first very slow. Instinctively, she'd assumed the tuck position, believing that this would propel her forwards with maximum speed. However, the piste was too deep, and even the wider skis started to sink. She then remembered that in such conditions the correct approach was to actually lean back, thereby allowing the front tips to come up side-by-side in order to use them collectively as one might a surfboard. She was even able to crouch just a little, thereby further decreasing the wind resistance. The speed whipped up in seconds as the skis responded without further hesitation. She now skimmed the surface as a water skier would the waves, making much more rapid progress as she traversed the most dangerous part of the mountain. Any mistake, now, on her part, and they would both die, long before she'd made it across.

Hurtling down the mountain, she followed an intercept course with Toby who was still polling frantically, but continuing to make lethally slow progress. Seconds before impact, he heard the swishing noise that her skis made on the surface of the slope. Just in time, he saw her swoop down heading straight for him. He braced himself for the impact, just as she did. Spreading her skis as wide as she was able, she ensured that they went around his, which were fortunately parallel and close together. She'd turned her face to one side so that the relatively broad area of the front of her legs and torso would absorb the force, assisted by the padded ski jacket and salopettes she wore. Though the collision winded her, she was able to grab him by the waist and hang on. The force so released, having checked the equal and opposite reaction, was then able to propel him along at a much faster speed than polling could bestow. She clung on tightly. They both moved forwards, the momentum allowing them to continue across the valley and onwards to the gentle downward slope, which lay just ahead.

The aquamarine sky framed the perfect snow scape. Surely, such a beautiful vista could harm no one. Sadly, the immaculate heavens remained neutral and therefore unable to influence the devastation that was now primed.

Knowing that head injuries represented a significant proportion of those who died at the hands of an avalanche, she rammed the helmet on his head as soon as she could. They continued across and slightly down as fast as the slope permitted. Both understood that getting across it was the priority, for their lives depended on it. The sides of the opposite ridge meant relative safety – perhaps. The avalanche's track would mean that most material and therefore most destructive force would be in the middle of the valley and this is where the speed of the avalanche would be at its highest. As an added bonus, here at the sides, a person was less likely to be buried, or if buried it would be invariably to a lesser depth.

Anyone who'd seen an avalanche, perhaps on television, or at a safe distance, would surely have remarked that it was a thing of beauty: its majestic descent and its scale while the deluge swept down the mountain, both humbling and awe-inspiring. Mountain dwellers would tell a very different tale. They would speak of the breath of white dragons as the powder cloud advanced at an obliterative rate, devouring everything and everyone in front of it. Experience dictated that anyone who witnessed this force of nature at close quarters would be forever entombed within its icy grasp.

The crack when it came was very loud. So loud, in fact, that it could only mean a crack in the world. This, for sure, was what it must have been, because the whole mountain started moving and was now coming straight for them.

For the third time since she'd met him, she gave out a heart-rending scream that had it come earlier, would immediately have triggered the avalanche. Initially, the angry god that had been awakened growled as he stirred and then came the roar that shook the earth and sky; now determined to wreak vengeance on the affairs of puny man. Within seconds a cataclysm of snow was on the move, harbouring a gargantuan force that nothing, and certainly not flesh and blood, could withstand.

She hugged him round the waist as they continued to ski down the mountain heading frantically for the edge of the avalanche track. Without doubt, they were too late, far too late, and taking too long – seemingly moving in slow motion – to even have a chance of outrunning the tsunami of snow racing to claim two foolish victims.

She screamed again. This was to be her last scream, knowing in that moment that this was 'it'. This was how it was always meant to be. Her mind flashed back to the day that she'd nearly skied off the edge of the precipice. In that moment, she could see that it was her destiny to come to such a brutal end on the icy crag. His act of saving her had in some way rendered his life now forfeit, and he was, therefore, required to settle his account in full – along with her.

The avalanche hit them with almighty ferocity. Seconds before, the powder cloud had immersed the pair so that neither of them could see. She knew that the torrent would be upon them before she could complete her thought. Avalanche training in Canada had taught her that she should lie back on the snow, attempting at all times to remain buoyant within its flow. In trying to remain on the surface, the person who was so caught was then advised to attempt backstroke, lying on one's back but with one's head facing the oncoming surge.

As soon as the deluge hit her, she deployed the airbags system. Pulling the cord, she realised that both their lives now depended on their presence. The pair of bright blue bags exploded as they went off, and formed within milliseconds either side of her back like a pair of angel's wings. The theory behind latest air bag technology was not to absorb the impact, for nothing could do this to a million tons of avalanche, but rather to keep the skier lighter and hence nearer the surface. She knew, inevitably, it would now inundate both of them. She was then compelled to think about how most people died when buried in this way – and that was asphyxiation – something that would occur within 15 minutes of complete immersion.

Leaning back on the airbags as far as she was able, she also attempted backstroke; fighting desperately to remain as near the surface as possible. Having done her best to cling to him, she knew that a human's puny grip would never be a match for a whole mountain of slush that was descending with illimitable violence. Still, she clung to him, as if the fate of the world, rather than just them, depended on her ability to do so. She felt him go just after her skis had been ripped away and her poles also. He, too, was swept downslope from her like a feather in a hurricane: her name was the last thing he cried as the deluge took him.

How long this continued she was not sure. The powder cloud was already moving past her but she realised then that there was enough snow heading for her to bury her without delay. She could only keep her head facing up the mountain while she became engulfed.

Thinking only at this point that she had to stay alive, because as they separated, she now represented his only chance of survival. Despite her efforts at remaining near the surface, she was soon covered. Tons of material buried her.

Within minutes the powder cloud started settling and the avalanche had passed, the cataract of snow having been funnelled with incomprehensible devastation down the valley that they'd been attempting to cross. Silence intervened and the quiet that arrived was the hush of death itself as it stalked the mountain covering two unmarked graves. The powder settled and the surface of the slope was restored, having been swept clear of ninety per cent of its coating. It formed a perfectly smooth surface but did not leave even a trace of their bodies.

****

Realising that she was still alive, her thoughts now were only for him. This single fact probably saved them both. Unrestrained panic would have killed someone trapped by such drifts within minutes by eating up precious oxygen. One who kept a cool head would have much longer to dig oneself out or await rescue. She'd managed to provide him with a helmet so that he would be protected from all but the most severe of head injuries. In addition she'd done her best to position herself higher up the mountain so that he may benefit from some shielding. Accepting that he did not have an avalanche protection system. She had neither the strength to carry one, nor the time to pass it to him. Wondering just how deep he would have been covered, she then considered if it were too optimistic to assume that he was still alive. She tried not to think of the cruellest thought: whether she'd have the energy to not only dig herself out, but also the time available to find him.

One of the airbags was still inflated and she used this to create some space around herself — literally breathing room. The bigger this volume, the longer she'd have available to dig. She knew that in any event she would only have a few minutes. This was the time the fluffy, pretty powder would take to set like concrete. She unzipped the backpack and at once activated the little torch. It created an eerie glow inside her icy prison. Doing her best to put panic to one side, she followed the training she'd been given in Canada. She then withdrew a long telescopic probe with a transponder on the end and most vitally, the folding shovel with a strong and sharp blade. She knew that if she were not able to get out, then the transponder would be traceable by the rescue services. Whether they would have time to access them was a moot point and inevitably she wondered if anyone would realise that they were there. If the rescue team's first destination was the chalet, then given that delay, they'd both be beyond rescue.

Using the probe, Alexis pierced the snow in the direction she thought was upwards. Mercifully it was thin enough for her to stand a chance of digging herself out. There was available to her a few golden minutes where the snow remained workable, after which it would assume a very different consistency.

Digging with urgency, she knew to dig forwards and downwards, as this was usually the easiest escape route. The drift was often weaker and thinner here, rather than directly over her head, where it would be much thicker and harder to work. She dug with a frenzy of someone who knew that another dear life, apart from her own, would be forfeit if she did not.

The angry god who'd been awakened in the mountains had wreaked his terrible vengeance and had now retired to slumber, once again – at least for now. In the silence that followed, the only noises she could hear were the sound of her own laboured breathing and the blade of the shovel as it tore frantically at the snow that was quickly setting, like the unbreachable barrier it would become if she slowed even for a minute. Though it was yielding to the shovel, she knew her rapidly weakening arms would have to continue if she were to save herself and then to do it all again, even if she were lucky enough to find him.

Alexis knew that she'd been fortunate. The airbags had certainly saved her life by keeping her higher in the torrent than she'd otherwise have been. Even when entombed they had given her vital breathing room and also working room to enable her to shift the material from in front to behind her as she started digging. She realised he'd been denied these two crucial advantages.

Eventually it appeared that the wall of snow was becoming lighter. This could only mean daylight. Working vigorously with the sharpened blade of the shovel, she attacked it with a fury. At last there was a flush of cold air and she knew she'd broken through. This in turn encouraged her to maintain her digging. Within seconds she was free, sitting for a minute in order to allow her weary arms some respite and breathe air that was fresh and vital.

She looked down the slope. The vision that awaited her was that of an immaculate virgin surface, which dazzled in the afternoon light looking perfect. How could it retain such forces that could sweep aside whole mountainsides and even forests? How could such an angelic thing be capable of killing so quickly?

She called to him but heard nothing: remembering that he'd been downslope of her when they'd separated. Taking into account that he was a heavier person without airbags, he would not only be further down the slope, but also covered to a greater depth.

She saw his ski poles. Pulling the plastic basket off the end of one of them, she intended to use this as a probe to attempt to find him in the blinding expanse. She frantically used it to probe the snow looking for something soft, and hopefully someone who was still breathing.

Thinking that she'd detected a soft spot, she renewed her frenzied digging efforts using her exhausted muscles, knowing only that she would not stop until they refused to work any longer. Moreover, she understood too, that she would not leave until she'd found him and told him the words that she now realised she'd been waiting all along to reveal.

Continuing to dig, she knew that panic was mounting within and she had to calm her racing thoughts in order to make the most of the time available to him. The digging was fruitless and once again she sat on the surface and called to him repeatedly. She knew that the rescue teams would be coming up from the village and that they'd be here very soon but nowhere near soon enough. The air pockets would only last so long.

Praying that he'd managed to eke out some breathing space, she hoped this might give him a little longer. Only then did her mind encompass an effective strategy. Removing her helmet, she called out to him again and then held her ear to the snow, the cold against the side of her face not registering. She desperately fought to try and stop herself from panting, her breathing appearing so loud as to confuse her attempts to locate him. Using the flat blade of the shovel like a drumstick, she beat the surface of the piste using a rhythm that he would know meant rescue – if only he were still able to respond.

Suddenly, she heard him, and also, in that moment, knew that he was very close – but how deep? She inserted the ski pole as far as she could, but it yielded no results. This could only mean that he was buried deeper than its length. She started digging again. Her arms were almost howling with pain and exhaustion. The cold and the thin air slowed her progress as they, too, conspired to sap her strength.

Digging a few feet, so as to form a small tunnel, she was able to crawl within and then used the pole again. Still nothing. Penetrating further into the covering of powder, she enlarged the hole so it did not collapse on her as she crawled inside once more. For the fourth time she used the pole and this time it felt as if it was going through and hitting something soft.

Alexis smiled when she discovered that he had grabbed the pole and was moving it from within his icy prison. Attacking the snow with fervour, she called to him repeatedly until her voice became hoarse and her very essence completely exhausted. She realised that the hole made by the probe would at least allow a little air to enter, and she did her best to rotate this so as to enlarge its passage and also allowed her weary muscles some respite. Eventually she broke through. Through the small gap, so formed, she could see his shiny blue eyes.

"Ouch, someone's been prodding me with a metal ski pole," he said as she saw him rubbing his shoulder through the small hole.

"Yes, and in a minute I'm going to hit you with a shovel – so stand back."

"I love it when you get angry. How did you know where I'd be?"

"I just knew of all the wonderful places and sights, this was more *you* than any of the others."

"You mean the chalet?" he asked mischievously.

"Yes, I wasn't referring to this snowy mountainside!" she confirmed.

She continued to dig frantically. Pausing for breath, she was able to speak. "By the way, on the rescue stakes it seems as if I am one up, now. That's if we don't count my trip off the stairs on your boat."

"And I am very glad that you are, though you obviously have a penchant for going down steep things very quickly."

"And I could say, you for getting stuck in tricky situations?"

The exhausted woman renewed her digging and eventually he was able to pull himself out through the hole and they both crawled through the tunnel to the entrance and fresh air. Toby was a little disorientated at first owing to lack of oxygen and his deep, cold incarceration. Within a couple of minutes, as he lay gasping, looking up at the blue sky, his head felt much clearer.

They both lay on the surface; he panting for oxygen and she because of the physical exertion she'd undertaken. In the distance could be heard the noise from the Ski-doos, which were venturing up from the village below. In addition a rescue helicopter approached, its rotors rhythmically cutting the air as it flew overhead from its base in the adjacent valley.

He gazed up at the blue sky and the glorious sun, just grateful to be alive and in the company of someone that he doubted he'd ever see again. She sat astride him and loosened his helmet. She kissed him.

"Are you all right? That was a bit of a close one. Good job I was just doing a spot of skiing. Avalanche surfing is my favourite sport."

For a few moments they just stared at each other as if they were seeing each other as who they really were for the very first time. No pretence, no deception and no lies, just two people who'd realised what was important, and what had grown between them, despite all else.

"Oh, I thought you'd come back for the Engineer's telephone number?"

She laughed. "Now, that's tempting, but not exactly. I came back for much more than that."

A pause then followed while each formulated words that were at that point more crucial than any that either had voiced in their lives before.

"Forgive me!" he began.

"Promise me!" she returned.

"Forgive me, I just couldn't find a way or the courage to tell you how special you are. I should have told you the moment I sat eyes on you. Can you possibly forgive me?"

"Promise me?"

She shook him by the lapels as her pretty smile rose resplendently like the sun that once again reigned over the beautiful and pristine slopes.

"Promise me!"

He paused for a moment but then realised what he'd been meaning to tell her for some time. Recent events had now clarified this precipitously. "Yes, okay I will, I promise, I'll love you forever."

"What? No, I meant, promise me you'll take me up in your balloon again."

"What, oh yes, of course, as soon as you'd like," he said with a question in his eyes.

"Well, I *was* going to settle for a balloon ride, but now you mention it, that sounds like a *much* better offer. That'll do nicely!"

She kissed him again and again. "Toby, this is me being spontaneous, by the way!"

"Glad to see it," he replied as he kissed her back, just as the Ski-doos ventured on to the newly created field of snow.

Chapter XVI

Cloak and Dagger

Two people walked side by side along the old Number 9 dock at Salford Quays. The cloudless night ensured that the temperature had dropped sharply, but their animated conversation meant that neither she nor he had noticed the cold. Only the brilliant disc of the ascendant moon accompanied them as they talked.

"Tell me?"

"Tell you what?"

"Was it you who brought down that avalanche on them?"

Miss Clancy looked shocked. "*Me*? How could you possibly think such a thing? That avalanche was *so* close, it almost killed them both. To even *contemplate* such a thing would have been a criminal act of irresponsibility."

"Sorry," he offered carefully, sensing he'd touched a nerve. "Only, you see, I was looking at her file. I saw that you'd highlighted that she'd done an avalanche survival course when she was in the Canadian Rockies."

"That was some years ago," she offered, without blinking.

"Ha!" he said, "So, it was you!"

"I've already given you my answer."

Detecting that, as regards to the questions, he was just getting into his stride. Therefore, she changed the subject quickly. "I'd been meaning to tell you how brave you were walking in on the Russian chap having lunch. I couldn't believe it when you closed the case!"

"Cruel bastard, there was no way he was going to have that case after what he put me through. I thought, 'I'm not going to waste a nice case on this creep'."

"Your first mission! They say the first one is always the hardest. And, as for the case, he won't be able to open it any time soon, and not without destroying it or at least chopping off two of your fingers!"

Swallowing hard, he gave a little shiver that had nothing to do with him suddenly noticing the cold wind.

"Mm, in that case I'd better keep looking behind me when I venture out."

"Don't worry. I think he'll be out of circulation, and will have many other things on his mind for the next few years. I'm certain that exacting revenge on you for closing that case won't be high on the list. In any event, now he's fallen from grace, many of his so-called 'friends' will probably turn on him, so that I suspect it's already all over for him – no matter what funds he's secreted away, for when he gets out."

Her voice, now almost smoky, dropped to its lowest register. "Okay then, as you did so well for your first mission, I thought we could go and do something, just the two of us?"

Swallowing hard again, but this time with very different thoughts coming to him, he wondered just what this might be. Looking appreciatively at her, and not for the first time, he noted the long legs, curvaceous chest, amazing figure and especially her sparkly eyes. The latter like two polished discs of mahogany. He was entranced watching them exhibiting chatoyancy, as their colour changed with the available light, with her mood and especially when reflecting the stars that were now shining over the Quays. "*Wow*, yes, let's. What have you got in mind?" he said, thinking that it wasn't his birthday for another month, though he'd always known that his banter and innuendo would wear her down, sooner or later.

"I thought we'd go and play cards."

Disappointment came upon him with an almost explosive deflation. "Play cards! I've given up cards since you rescued me."

"Good job, too, you were a lousy card player. We'd been watching you lose your shirt for days. In fact, even if that bugger hadn't been cheating, I still think you'd have lost."

"Yes, thank you for that."

"Truth never hurts as much as a good lie," she advised.

"Yes, I'll have to write that down and think about it. I was just wondering?"

"Yes," she said suspiciously, having realised that deflecting the conversation had only brought temporary respite.

"Talking of surveillance, I was looking at the video footage of the avalanche. You know it started *just* at the right time?"

"*Really*? How so?"

"I reckon if it started fifteen seconds earlier, then they both would have been killed. I reckon it would have been goodnight Vienna," he concluded.

"Wow! That is so lucky, don't you think?"

"Do you think a sniper could have started that avalanche?"

"No, nobody could have done that at that range. It would require one hell of a marksman."

"Not even with the *Accuracy International* sniper rifle," he postulated. "I suppose it was too cold anyway. Nobody could use a frozen sniper rifle in those conditions."

"No, they make an AW, *Arctic Warfare,* which is winter proof," she offered nonchalantly.

"Then, of course, you'd need a really good sniper's scope. Probably a *Zeiss*?"
"No, I think maybe a *Schmidt and Bender* with variable magnification," she suggested, thoughtfully.

"Really?" he clarified whimsically, before pausing.

"But then, there'd be the distance. It must have been over 800 metres, I guess," he wondered.

"No, I reckon much nearer the kilometre, maybe further than that."

"Extraordinary. But surely, just one shell couldn't trigger that whole thing?"

"Well, given a truly wonderful shooter, he'd then have to select a cartridge very carefully, He'd have to chamber a *Raufoss Mark 211 High Explosive* round that was aimed and timed to perfection. Then, don't forget, you'd need a muzzle brake on the rifle to cut down on recoil, jump and flash, in case the skiers had noticed it. Of course, I expect they'd be too busy just trying to get across and to safety. Even a trained ear wouldn't pick out the shot in that expanse, under those conditions."

"*Accuracy International*, is that an English sniper rifle, the choice of all British forces and NATO? Is that not the type of rifle you use?"

"I have been known to," she admitted, coyly.

"And a range of a thousand metres? I've seen you hit targets at that distance?"

Detecting that it was time to move the conversation on again, she said, "Anyway, I am sure you'll learn much more about these things. I believe you'll be starting your sniper and gun training next week? We'll make a man of you yet."

"Actually, I was hoping you were going to do that tonight."

"No, I can't see a high probability of that. In fact I think it's a negative probability."

"What's a negative probability?"

"It's a chilly day in Hell, kind of thing," she confirmed.

"That unlikely, eh? Oh, yes I see. Well, can I ask then?"

She groaned inwardly, for she had a sixth sense about his next line of questioning.

"You told Alexis that you're in love with Toby. I read it in the report. Is that true?"

"No, let's just say that when you have a losing hand, you have to make every one of those cards count for maximum effect. When you understand that, you'll be a better card player."

"Oh, I see," he began, but didn't really follow her logic, "So, does that mean you're not?"

"I believe I answered that question."
"The other thing," he began, as she agonised again, wondering what searching line of enquiry he was about to switch to, "you told Alexis that she would be our last mission. Is that true?"

"I believe I've answered that, too," she confirmed with a pleasant nod in his direction.

Sensing that he wasn't getting very far, he tried a different tack. "Well, will you at least tell me your name!"

"Of course I will, Tim, it's not all cloak and dagger stuff, you know."

"Only, you promised, if I signed up, that you'd tell me your name, and I am *still* waiting."

"I lied."

"About what?"

"About that. Maybe after your next mission?"

"But I can't keep calling you Miss Clancy, now can I?"

"Oh, yes, that'll be fine," she confirmed before kissing him gently.

His heart fluttered, his legs trembled and his throat became dry as the cold wind whipped along the Quays. It was to be several long minutes before he was able to speak again. "Well, in that case, here's to the next mission," he managed, struggling to keep his voice steady.

"Come on, I'll let you buy me a drink."

"It'll be my pleasure, Miss Clancy. Surely, I can't call you 'Miss Clancy' in the bar, now can I?" he asked, sensing that she'd have to reveal her first name sooner rather than later.

"Oh, don't worry, they all call me that in there. Just don't get any ideas like this is a date, or anything like that."

"I'd never do such a thing with a woman who can shoot as well as you."

She laughed and, as they got to the pub, "Even at 1200 metres… and I can see you are catching on very quickly."

In the pub, he raised a glass as he tried not to stare at those mesmerising eyes that noticed so much and revealed other facets to her character – only when she was ready.

"Here's to our next mission, the next Horizon."

"I'll drink to that, Tim," offered, Miss Clancy.

** THE END **